The summer had started
with such brightness, such promise.

Ellen's first terrible grief after her mother's death had begun to settle into an ache that could be borne. There was a marvelous art class being offered through the schools, and she and Clarisse were going to attend it together. Everything had been wonderful.

Then Randy came home from school and the whole world started to crumble and fall apart. . . .

THE BLESSING DEER

LOIS T. HENDERSON

THE BLESSING DEER
© 1980 Lois T. Henderson

First printing, September 1980
Second printing, April 1983
Third printing, April 1986

Published by David C. Cook Publishing Co., Elgin, IL 60120
Printed in the United States of America
ISBN 0-89191-244-4
LC 79-57215

To my grandchildren
Robert Michael Nichols
and
Lisa Marie Nichols

Preface

Manitoulin Island is a real island, the largest fresh-water island in the world, located in the northern waters of Lake Huron in Ontario. I want to express my gratitude to all the residents of the island who have taught me to know it and to love it. My thanks go especially to Dorothy and Goldie Tustian and to the entire Allan Little family for all that they have shared with me during the past eighteen summers. My indebtedness is unlimited to Isobel and Dane Wandabense for their encouragement and their help with this manuscript. I also want to express my appreciation to Ruth Curry for her generous assistance.

Although this story takes place in a real location, the characters are fictitious, and any resemblance to persons, living or dead, is purely coincidental.

1

"But, Ellen, school starts in two weeks. You can't go to Manitoulin Island *now*."

Ellen Ramsey looked at her father, feeling almost desperate. She had to make him understand how she felt. She simply *had* to.

"I'm not talking about a vacation, daddy. I'm talking about going there to live."

She should have known he would look like that, bewildered and anxious. Not angry. Maybe if he got angry like other kids said their fathers did, she could fight this thing better.

"I want to live there," she repeated, hearing the stubbornness creep into her voice. Well, stubbornness was better than crying, and heaven knows she had cried enough the past few days to last for six months.

"But, why, darling? Why now?"

"Daddy, listen," Ellen began and then stopped. She didn't think she could ever come up with the right words, the words that would make it clear to him that she had to get away from Washington, that she would simply die if she had to stay in this hate-filled, prejudice-ridden city one more week. One more day, really. She'd like to leave tonight, this minute, even before dinner was finished.

Her father waited patiently for her to go on, but when she remained silent he looked up with a questioning glance. When she still said nothing, he looked calmly at his plate. "You've learned to make a really good salmon loaf," he said in an even voice. "I'd never have believed you'd turn into a cook like this by the time you were fourteen."

"We made salmon loaf last year in homemaking," Ellen said dully. She didn't add, *And I never would have had to learn this soon if mom hadn't died in that crazy, insane accident last year.* But the words were in her mind, mixed bitterly with the memory of the senseless tragedy that had changed her life. That was when she had first begun to think that a city must be crazy or evil when drunk drivers could careen up onto sidewalks where innocent people were walking.

"Now," her father went on, almost as though

there had been no interruption, "try to tell me why you've suddenly decided that you want to leave me and go to Canada to live."

The tears were spilling abruptly onto Ellen's cheeks before she could stop them. "Not leave *you,* daddy," she choked out. "I don't want to leave you. But I can't stand to stay here."

"Why?" he asked in the voice he used to lecture in his theology classes at the university. "Why haven't you told me before? A person doesn't just decide in a day that she wants to move away—especially to another country."

"It wasn't just in a day," she said, wishing she could stop crying. "It's been for a long time."

"Ever since your mother died?"

She didn't answer immediately, because she wanted to be completely honest with him. Had she thought of going to live with Aunt Betty and Uncle Archie Ludlow right after mom had died? Aunt Betty had told her after the funeral that she would be welcome on the island anytime she wanted to come, but it hadn't really meant anything then.

"No," she said at last. "I didn't—I couldn't have left you then. You would have been so alone."

Her father slowly buttered a piece of bread and then looked up with a slight smile. "But now you think I won't be alone? Because of Frances?"

Ellen's answer was hot and quick. "Daddy, that's not fair. I never even thought of Frances. Not for one minute. I—" But her voice slowed as her mind really registered what she was saying. "I—I guess," she faltered, "maybe Frances does come into this in a way. I mean, I feel different about leaving you now. You wouldn't be so alone now that you have Frances."

"Well, I don't exactly 'have' her," Mr. Ramsey said dryly. "I've only known her about three months."

"As a friend," Ellen said.

"Okay, as a friend. You're not jealous? Honestly, Ellen?"

She shook her head vehemently, her long hair flying out. "No, honestly. Frances is nice." Ellen's tears were almost dried up in her earnest desire to convince her father. "I'm glad you and she are friends. You needed someone, and I'm only a kid."

Her eyes filled again. He was really making it terribly hard, and it wasn't because he was unreasonable or selfish. It was only because he loved her.

"Don't cry," he said. "You've cried so much lately. It seems your eyes have been red for days. Can't you tell me?"

For a minute she only shook her head and looked down at her plate. How could she tell him? How could she bear to put it into words—the hot humiliation of last week or the terrible, terrible anger she felt—not toward any individual person but toward a country that let people hate without reason until friends turned into enemies?

"Let me guess," he said at last. "It has something to do with Clarisse."

"How did you know?" she asked astonished.

"I didn't. I said I was only guessing. Is she mad at you?"

"Oh, daddy, it isn't 'mad.' It's a thousand times worse than that."

His voice took on the professional solemnity again. "Ellen, you knew when you and Clarisse started to be friends that it might be sticky. It isn't always easy for white and black kids to be close friends."

"Of course, I knew. I still know. But Clarisse and I were friends because we were in the same homeroom for three years—because we liked studying together and laughing together—because we took that art course together—because we're so much alike. What difference did it make that she's black and I'm white?"

Mr. Ramsey shrugged. "No difference to me," he said. "Evidently none to you. And I thought none to Clarisse. So what's the hang-up?"

Ellen struggled with the words and they came out badly. "Clarisse doesn't like me anymore," she said.

"Oh, come on, Ellen. People don't just stop liking their best friends. What makes you think she doesn't like you?"

"Because I'm white."

"Nonsense! You've always been white, and she

liked you before."

"Daddy," Ellen said desperately, "you don't know what it's like. You don't know how it is to be black and live in Washington and have people look down on you and—and be hateful. I understand why Clarisse feels the way she does. You can't blame her. It isn't her fault."

"Agreed!" Mr. Ramsey said. "But it isn't your fault, either, is it? Have *you* ever been hateful?"

"You just don't understand, daddy," Ellen wailed.

His voice was patient. "I'm trying to, Ellen. But you've got to help me. Why has Clarisse changed?"

Ellen's mind flew back to the beginning of the summer, the summer that had started off with such a brightness, such promise. Her first terrible grief for her mother was gentling itself into something that could be borne, there was a marvelous art class being offered through the schools, and she and Clarisse were going to attend it together. Everything had been wonderful, and then Randy came home from school and the whole world started to crumble and fall apart.

"I think Randy—" Ellen began.

"Clarisse's brother?"

"Yes. He came home from college and he was different. And he—well, he changed Clarisse."

"How 'changed' her?"

"Last week," Ellen said slowly, painfully. "Last week the art teacher laughed at Clarisse's work. I tried to talk to Clarisse, but she turned her back on me and told me to go away. 'What do you care, you white honkey,' she said. 'Randy's right. All you whites are alike. Blacks 'n whites just can't be friends.' "

The bitter shock of that moment made all the rumors Ellen had heard at school about race riots seem real. She knew some of that fear must show now in her eyes.

She watched her father's jaw tighten until a knot of muscle jumped along the edge of it.

When he spoke at last, his voice was very soft. "Clarisse is only one girl, Ellen. Aren't there other girls?"

"But not like Clarisse. And, besides, if this place—this country—can do things like this to Clarisse and me, it's not where I want to be!" Ellen said, her voice breaking. "I can't stand it, daddy. I just can't. Sometimes I think if I can't get away to where things are different, I'll die."

She put her head down on the table, and sobs shook her until she could hardly breathe. She felt her father's hand on her head, but he didn't say anything for a few minutes. The silence grew and expanded until Ellen thought it might just burst like a huge balloon.

When Mr. Ramsey spoke at last, his words were so unexpected that Ellen wasn't sure she'd heard him correctly.

"Does Aunt Betty know you're planning to

come?" he asked.

Ellen's heart jerked in her chest. He wasn't saying "no" right away.

"No," she said, her voice muffled against her arms. "Oh, I write to them, you know that, and she asks me to come. I've thought about it a lot lately, but I haven't said anything."

"I've thought about it, too," Mr. Ramsey said, and Ellen's head shot up abruptly.

"You have?" she cried. "Why haven't you ever said anything?"

He shrugged and spread his hands. "I'm not really sure. Your Aunt Betty keeps writing that you'd be better off up there with them, but I can't get over the feeling that this is where you belong. And it wouldn't be easy to give you up."

"It wouldn't be easy to leave you," she said breathlessly, "but, oh, daddy, it would be so perfect on the island. It's clean and quiet and beautiful, and people, well they aren't prejudiced against each other."

"Don't be so sure about that, Ellen," Mr. Ramsey said. "People are people, and prejudice isn't limited—"

But she broke in rudely, refusing to let him say the words she didn't want to hear. "I won't even listen, daddy, because it's not true. I've been there. I *know*."

"You haven't lived there, Ellen. You can't know for sure about any place until you've lived there."

"I know," she repeated stubbornly. "I just know."

He shook his head, looking a little helpless. He opened his mouth to say something, then evidently changed his mind and shut it again.

Ellen spoke eagerly, using every persuasion she knew. "I'd love to go, daddy. I'd love to live with the Ludlows." The thought flashed through her mind that it would be almost like having mom again, because she and Aunt Betty had been twins, but she felt the words might hurt her father so she didn't say them. "And you know how I feel about the island. I'd be happy there, I know I would. And nothing could hurt me. Not like here."

"How about the water?" he said. "The boys go out in boats in all kinds of weather, and I know you'd want to go along. I don't think I'd ever sleep peacefully again."

She actually laughed a little. "Oh, come on, daddy. You let me walk on the streets of Washington. The North Channel couldn't possibly be as dangerous as that."

"With that maniac, Sam, at the tiller? I've ridden with him. He may be a year older than you, Ellen, but he's irresponsible. You said so yourself when you were there two years ago. Even Uncle Archie admits that. Sam's different from his brothers."

She dismissed Sam with a flip of her hand. "Oh, Sam!" she said disdainfully. "He wouldn't want me out in a boat with him anyhow. And you could trust

Dave."

Her father smiled. "Well, you're right there. I could trust Dave."

Ellen smiled too, thinking of Dave, who was nineteen and so good-looking that it was really a shame he was her cousin. And then her father spoke again.

"You'd really leave your own country?" he said, but not accusingly.

"I'd like to leave it forever," she answered and was surprised at how hard her voice sounded. "I can't feel very loyal to a place that—where—" She faltered, unable to find the words.

Her father didn't answer. He seemed to be thinking of something else. When he spoke, his voice was very serious. "I don't want to sound preachy," he said, "but there's one thing I'm terribly concerned about. If you really go, what about your . . . spiritual growth, if I may use a heavy term? The Ludlows, wonderful as they are, are not church people, the way we are."

"Aunt Betty goes to church," she protested.

"But Uncle Archie and the bigger boys don't. I don't know how that would influence you. I'd worry about that."

Gathering up her courage, Ellen said the words she had thought so many times recently but had never believed she would dare say to her father. "Besides, I don't feel as churchy as you think I do. I think the Christian church is phony! They preach one thing and practice something else. Clarisse and I wouldn't be welcome in the same church, even though we believe the same."

"Oh, come on, Ellen. Lots of churches serve mixed groups."

"How many blacks are there in our church?" she demanded, and saw, with satisfaction, that he had no answer for that. At least no satisfactory answer.

"So you see," she went on, taking advantage of her small victory, "even if I stayed here, I might not go to church. Not so often, anyway. And when I did, I'd only go to please you."

Her father was silent, then he said slowly, "I'm sorry, Ellen. I had no idea how you felt."

She just shook her head, half sorry she had been so frank, half relieved that she had finally expressed her feelings.

"I won't make any demands about church attendance," Mr. Ramsey said, "if you feel so strongly about it. But I hope you won't object if I pray that you change your mind."

He was smiling and she tried to match his warmth with a smile of her own.

"I won't object," she said. "Not that you'd stop if I did."

"I will ask you to make one promise, if you go," Mr. Ramsey said. "Only one, but I'll expect you to keep it."

"What?" she asked cautiously. A promise wasn't to be taken lightly.

"That you'll never go to sleep at night without praying. That you'll turn to God for guidance in everything. Could you promise me that, Ellen?"

"You don't have to ask me that, daddy. It isn't that I've stopped believing in God or Jesus or anything like that. You ought to know I'd pray."

His expression didn't change. "I'd still like your promise," he said softly.

She felt an ache in her throat. He cared so much, and it wasn't his fault that she was mixed-up and angry, bitter, and hurt. "I promise, daddy," she said solemnly, like a vow. "No matter how I feel about anything else. And if we both pray, it will make it seem as though we're still close, won't it?"

He nodded. "Close to each other and to God. I can't tell you *how* to pray, Ellen. I only know that for myself I couldn't have survived without it."

"Why don't you call Aunt Betty right now?" he said abruptly. "After all, there's always the possibility that it wouldn't suit them to have an extra girl when they already have four boys."

She stared at him, her mouth open. He had actually given his permission. He hadn't just said so in that many words, but that's what he meant. She threw her arms around his neck.

"Oh, Daddy, I never dreamed you'd let me go."

He hugged her hard and then pushed her toward the telephone. "Go ahead," he said. "Call before I change my mind—or come to my senses."

She dialed the familiar number. Far away the

telephone buzzed with a blurred sound, and Ellen felt her heart jumping in her throat. *What if they weren't home? Or what if—in spite of the repeated invitations—Aunt Betty didn't really want her to come?*

"Hello?" It was Aunt Betty, sounding as close as though she were only next door. Even her voice was like mom's.

"Aunt Betty? This is Ellen." The words came out chokingly, forced past the knot in her throat.

"Ellen? What's the matter, darling? Are you all right? You sound funny."

"Aunt Betty," Ellen said, saying the words fast and desperately, before her courage failed her. "Aunt Betty, could I come and stay with you? For all the time, I mean. Not just a visit."

Ellen didn't know exactly what kind of a response she expected, but she hadn't even hoped for the warmth and promptness of her aunt's answer.

"Of course you can! We'd love it. Will your father let you?"

"Yes, he says—he says I can come." Ellen was afraid to look at her father, afraid maybe he'd change his mind, even now.

"Darling, it would be marvelous. Let me talk to your father. Could you get here before school starts?"

"Yes, I can come as soon as I'm packed. Here, talk to daddy. Oh, Aunt Betty, thank you."

She handed the telephone to her father.

She went over to the big chair and curled up in a tight little ball, hardly hearing her father's smooth, measured voice. She didn't have to worry anymore. They would take care of everything—her aunt and her father. All that mattered was that she was free to go, free to escape from Clarisse's bitterness and the loneliness that waited for her every day when she came home from school to an empty apartment.

She was suddenly aware that her father was no longer talking. She looked up to see him watching her with an odd expression on his face.

She jumped up from the chair and flung herself into his arms.

He held her closely and then he spoke quietly. "One more thing, Ellen. I can't give my permission for you to leave me—to leave America—forever. A year. I'll give you a year to see how it works out. And then we'll talk again. Okay?"

She nodded her head violently. Anything. She'd agree to anything just so she could go.

"Okay," she said. "A year." And then she said the words that were so hard to say that she wondered how people in novels and movies could say them so glibly. "I love you, daddy," she said. "I really do."

2

The plane banked for the beginning of the landing pattern, and Ellen, her heart pounding high in her throat from excitement, leaned to look out of the small window. Her last real view of the ground had been at Toronto. Her father had flown that far with her, seeing her safely onto the smaller plane for Sudbury. When the plane left the ground at Toronto, the city had stretched beneath her, just as it had in Washington, with streamers of smoke, clusters of industries, all the reminders of the sort of life Ellen was eager to leave. *It'll be different here in Sudbury,* she thought with a touch of contentment, and was immediately shocked to see the scars and wounds on the earth caused by nickel mining. Strange how she always forgot! She had ridden past Sudbury half-a-dozen times in her life, but always when she was back home she forgot the acid smoke, the death of vegetation, the ugliness of the nickel mining. She could only remember Uncle Archie's farm and the wide stretches of water where sometimes you could go for a full day in a small boat and see no one else.

Well, it didn't matter what was here in Sudbury, anyhow, because it would only be a few minutes until they'd be on their way to the island. She wondered who would meet her. Uncle Archie and Aunt Betty, of course, and Andrew would be along, because he was only six and too little to be left at home. But maybe the other three boys would think it was silly to come and meet a girl cousin, especially a nineteen year old like Dave. And Sam—well, it was hard to tell about Sam. When they were little, he had been fun to be with. But two years ago when she was here for her holiday, he had been teasing and "ornery," as Uncle Archie said. Maybe he'd be nicer now. Twelve-year-old Phillip, so much like Dave, would undoubtedly think a trip to Sudbury was a waste of time, when there was fishing and swimming to be done in the few days before school started.

The ground bumped under the plane's wheels and Ellen's stomach lurched up to meet her wildly beating heart and then settled down again. She ran her hands down over her long, dark hair, hoping it was smooth in spite of the nap she had taken a short time before.

It seemed like an hour before she was finally walking down the steps to the ground, her eyes scanning the small group of people gathered to meet the plane. At first she didn't see anyone who belonged to her, but then a frantically waving arm caught her attention, and it was Aunt Betty. For a second, Ellen thought she couldn't breathe. In spite of all her anticipation, she really had forgotten how terribly much Aunt Betty and Mom looked alike. Aunt Betty's hair was short and curly and she was a little plumper and wore more casual clothes. Ellen's mother had been slimmer and more sophisticated looking, but otherwise, they were identical. Seeing the beloved face with eyes so much like Ellen's own, and the warm, wide smile, was, all of a sudden, more than Ellen could bear. Her eyes filled with tears because it was almost like seeing mom alive again—alive and happy and no accident or loneliness anywhere.

Ellen ran to the waiting arms. Aunt Betty held her very tightly, and her voice was shaky when she said, "Hi, sweetie. It's about time you got here. We couldn't have endured waiting much longer."

And then Uncle Archie had her in a great bear hug, and Andrew was grinning shyly at her and even letting her kiss him. She stopped, breathless, certain the greetings were over when a tall, slender boy grabbed her in a quick hug and dropped a kiss on her cheek.

"Hi, Ellen. Welcome to the north!"

It was Dave. She simply couldn't believe it—first, that he was here, second, that he had grown so tall and was so incredibly good-looking, and third, that he hadn't even been embarrassed to kiss her in public. He must have grown up a lot! She had always adored Dave, but she had never dreamed he would turn out like *this*.

"Hi," she said, blinking away the tears and smiling at her tall cousin. "I didn't think *you'd* come to meet *me*."

"Mom made me," he said, but his grin gave him away.

"Couldn't have made him stay home," said Uncle Archie comfortably. "Isn't every day a fellow gets a new sister and an old cousin all rolled into one."

"Actually," Dave said, "they brought me along to carry luggage. Dad's on holiday."

"Phillip and Sam stayed home," Aunt Betty said. "They had chores, and besides, it would have crowded us pretty much."

Andrew pulled at her skirt. "They're going fishing," he said. "If they get enough bass, we'll have fish for supper. Mom said you'd like that."

"I'd love it," Ellen said fervently. She turned to her aunt, stabbed again by the startling resemblance to her mother. "Oh, Aunt Betty, it's *good* to be here. Thank you so much for letting me come."

Aunt Betty was indignant. *"Letting* you? We've felt this is where you belonged ever since—well, for a long time. It's the easiest and nicest way to get a girl in the family that I know."

"Don't get any ideas that it's going to be all roses," Dave said. "I've been doing research on sisters, and they don't get half as many privileges as cousins."

"Oh?" Ellen said, delighted with the easy way she and Dave were falling back into the old routine of mock insult and teasing.

"Cousins get entertained. Sisters do dishes, make beds, and clean fish!"

"Dishes and beds, yes," Ellen said. "But cleaning fish is man's work. If there just happen to be any men around, of course."

Dave pretended to make a fist, and she ducked away in mock alarm.

Andrew watched solemnly. "Is he mad at her?" he asked his mother.

Aunt Betty laughed. "They're teasing, honey. You'll see—Ellen and Dave won't ever get mad."

Was there the very slightest emphasis on the word "Dave"? Ellen wondered. Her excitement had made her overly sensitive, it seemed, so that she seemed to be aware of every sound and color and movement. *Does this mean that maybe Sam is still being "ornery"? Oh, well, look at how Clarisse and Randy used to fight when Randy was younger.*

THE BLESSING DEER

Fighting is normal in families. As long as I have Dave for a friend, she thought serenely, *I can handle anything else.*

The two-hour ride to the island passed in a flash and yet it seemed to take forever. There was so much to say, so much to get caught up on, but Ellen was so eager for the first sight of the island that it seemed she couldn't wait. Then, there it was. After the hills on the mainland and the flatness of LaCloche Island, they were crossing the causeway to Manitoulin and Ellen could see the pile of coke at the shipping dock, the strange, narrow little bridge that swung aside to let boats through, and the town, Little Current, sprawling in its haphazard way behind the harbor that held such elegant boats in the summer months when the tourists were "cluttering up" the island. Everything looked dear and familiar, and Ellen just looked and looked.

There were only three or four main streets, but there were stores and houses and churches and a bank, and it was all anyone needed. Since it was several miles to Uncle Archie's farm, they didn't come into town every day, but Little Current was the hub of this small world, and Ellen loved it.

They didn't even stop but headed right out the road toward the farm. For several miles they followed the new, curving highway, then turned into a narrow, unpaved road. The trees grew close to the berm, and Ellen felt the vast loneliness all around her. It was a little scary—it always was—

28

but oh, the lovely silence, the beautiful bigness of it. The island was more than a hundred miles long—the biggest fresh-water island in the world—with only about eleven thousand people. There was room to breathe here, room to grow and not have to push anyone around.

The weathered gray barn was the first thing she saw as they topped the last hill, and her breath almost stopped in her throat. Everyone seemed to sense how she was feeling, and even Andrew was quiet as they turned the last curve and went in through the rutted driveway to the square, shingled house under the huge old pine trees.

"Oh," Ellen said, and then a little foolishly because she wanted to say something terribly important, "there's old Shep. He doesn't even look any older."

"Welcome home, honey," Aunt Betty said.

Uncle Archie braked to a stop and turned to smile at Ellen. "We'll do our best to turn you into a Ludlow," he said. "Seems already like you're just one of us."

"I feel it, too," Ellen said a little breathlessly, ignoring the tiny stab of guilt she felt at being so quick to forget she was a Ramsey.

Phillip and Sam were down by the shore, working at the fish table, and they both waved and Phillip yelled that they'd be up in a minute. Sam only said "Hi" but Ellen was too excited and happy to even think about it.

Oh, the smell of the air! There wasn't anything like it in the whole world, she felt. Not anything anywhere. There was the dark, spicy smell of the pines, warmed in the sun, the smell of the water that couldn't really be defined—it was part fish and part weed smell and part something else altogether. And there was the farm smell—strong and horsey and exciting.

"Oh," Ellen said, "I think I'm going to cry."

"You do," Dave threatened, "and you carry your own suitcases into the house."

She laughed then, and the bad minute was over. They showed her into the room that was to be hers. It was in the front of the house, and the lake could be seen from her window. It was the room that had been Sam's. Dave and Phil had always shared a room, not because they were near in age, but because they were so alike in temperament and interest. They both thought that getting up at 5 A.M. to go fishing was normal and sane, and by rooming together they didn't bother anyone else. But Sam had had this room, and Andrew, being the baby, had the room nearest his parents.

"Doesn't Sam mind?" Ellen asked, gazing with delight at the new bedspread, pink and feminine, and the ruffled white curtains at the window.

"Not at all," said Uncle Archie just a shade too heartily, and Ellen saw Dave clap a quick hand over Andrew's mouth, which had been opening for an eager comment.

"Sam spends so much time in front of the tv," Aunt Betty said briskly, "that he'll never know where he's sleeping."

But they weren't telling the whole truth and Ellen could sense it.

I hope Sam won't get all uptight, she thought. But there wasn't any more time to think of it just then, as Aunt Betty insisted on showing off the changes in the house since her last visit—the color tv, the new cupboards in the kitchen, the broad new porch that had such a breathtaking view of the lake.

After she had made her grand tour, Aunt Betty suggested that she start unpacking while supper got under way, and then everyone could relax at once.

Contentedly, feeling really happy, Ellen went to the room that was to be hers. She closed the door only long enough to slip into the jeans and shirt she had packed on the top of her bag, and then she opened the door again, wanting everyone to know that she wasn't trying to be alone, that visitors of any age and size would be welcome.

She heard the sound of the boys coming up from the lake and Aunt Betty's exclamation of pleasure over the size of the catch. Oh, yummy, that meant fresh crisp-fried fish for supper. There was just nothing anywhere in the world that was any better. Not the most elegant seafood restaurant in Washington could match it.

In just a minute a noise at the door made her look up, and there was Phil, smiling his shy smile that made her think of Dave and Uncle Archie. Phil was going to be tall, too, but right now he was at that awkward stage, all hands and feet—too big to be little and too young to be a big boy.

"Hi, Phil," she said. "Did I hear talk out in the kitchen about fish?"

"Yep. We got twelve. Both got our limit."

"Oh, great. I haven't had fresh bass for two years."

Phil grinned. "Actually, Sam got seven and I only got five. But it evens out and no one can know."

"Where *is* Sam?" Ellen asked over her shoulder, putting folded underwear in the drawer.

There was a minute's silence and she glanced around in surprise, just in time to see a pink flush of embarrassment on Phil's face. "He—he went back down to the lake," Phil stuttered. "Thought he could get in a quick swim before we eat."

He didn't even stop to say hello, Ellen thought, with a sort of sinking feeling in her chest. *He really is mad because I got his room.*

But she didn't want to embarrass Phil by saying anything, and besides, what was there to say? She had, after all, just moved in and moved Sam out. But she was hoping so much that everyone would be glad to see her. It was going to be hard if Sam had made up his mind not to like her. Sam was stubborn,

Uncle Archie always said. Stubborn as a mule.

"Water cold yet?" Ellen asked, her voice muffled as she bent over her suitcases.

"Not much," Phil said, relieved that she wasn't going to make an issue of it. "Colder than August, but it'll still be good for swimming for another couple of weeks. If you're used to it, that is."

"I'll try it even if I'm not used to it," Ellen said. "Every day till school starts."

"That's only three days," Phil said dolefully.

Ellen's heart jumped. The idea of a new school was the most terrifying thing of all. Sam would be nearest in age and grade. If only he'd be friendly, it wouldn't be so bad. Well, she'd just have to work it out.

But when Sam came in for supper, his greeting was so abrupt and gruff that she had a feeling of almost total panic for a minute. This wasn't some silly baby grudge that he'd get over in three or four days; Sam was really set against her.

Her eyes flew to Aunt Betty's, and there was encouragement there, but no promise of an easy victory. Aunt Betty might love her a great deal, but Sam would have to be reckoned with—and with no help from anyone. After all, Aunt Betty could make him be polite, but she couldn't make him like his American cousin unless he wanted to.

When bedtime came, Ellen was almost too tired for prayers, but she had promised, so she tried to marshal her thoughts into some semblance of order.

"Thank you, Lord, for letting me come," she whispered at last, "and, dear God, please change Sam into a friend."

3

"It wouldn't be so bad if it were raining," moaned Phil. "I could almost stand it if it were raining."

"Even then, it would be rotten," said Sam.

"Oh, come on," Aunt Betty said, "School isn't all that bad. You'll give both Andrew and Ellen the wrong impression."

"Girls and first graders aren't supposed to understand," Sam said. "They're both dumb."

Dave laughed. "The way you were hanging around Mary Ann Trevor down at the dock yesterday, I'd never think you thought girls were so dumb."

"Aw, shut up," Sam snapped.

"Don't say 'shut up' to each other," Aunt Betty said, but anyone could see she was saying it automatically. Her worried glance came to rest on Ellen's face.

"Don't pay any attention to the boys," she said encouragingly. "School is going to be fun. You'll like it. It probably won't be much different than it was in Washington."

"Right," agreed Ellen cheerfully, trying to ignore the nervous fluttery feeling in her stomach. "School is school anywhere in the world, I guess. Only, Phil is right. A day like this ought to come in vacation time."

"Sometimes September's the nicest month on the island," Aunt Betty said. "Come on now, everybody, get ready. The bus'll be at the end of the lane in just a few minutes. And I don't care how ghastly it seems, one of you stick with Andrew until he's on the bus that goes to his school! I mean it. And one of you with Ellen. At least until she's found some girl she knows."

"I'll take care of Andy," Phil said. "Only tell him he has to mind me."

"Don't worry about me, Aunt Betty," Ellen said quickly. It would just be too utterly horrible to have any of the boys have to sit with her on the bus. Nice as Dave was, it would look pretty weird to have a guy have to sit with his cousin, especially when she was only in ninth grade and he was in thirteenth. And Sam, well, she'd rather be alone anytime, and

Phil would have his hands full with Andrew.

"Mary Ann's already on the bus when it gets here," Dave said. "She'll look out for Ellen."

"Did you ask her to?" Sam said quickly, his voice more angry than curious.

"She offered down at the dock yesterday," Dave said quietly. "She'd have probably rather told you, but you were too busy trying to drown yourself or look like some fool hero—one of the two."

Sam got red but had the grace to look embarrassed.

"Good," Aunt Betty said, her voice sounding relieved. "Mary Ann's a nice girl. You know her, don't you, Ellen?"

"Uh huh. We met down at the dock when we went swimming. She's new here though, isn't she?"

"No, they've lived in Little Current for years, but they just moved out to the farm next door a year ago. You'll like her."

"So does Sam," said Andrew. "He's always taking her something."

"You talk too much," Sam said, but he didn't sound angry anymore.

If Mary Ann could put Sam in a good mood, Ellen reflected, *she must be special.*

There was a quick flurry of good-byes, last-minute warnings about watching out for Andrew, and then the five were out of the house at last and racing up the lane.

THE BLESSING DEER

The air was absolutely gorgeous, Ellen decided. There just wasn't another word. Although it was still cool, the sun came warmly through the openings between the branches of trees. The clean, fresh smell of early country morning was intoxicating, and it seemed to Ellen that if this place gave her nothing more than lovely smells, it might almost be enough.

After she had gone to bed the past few nights, even the prayers had not been able to prevent some bad minutes of homesickness for her father. And when Sam had been particularly rude, there had been periods when she had longed for the comfort of being the only child with no competition. But now, in the pine-sweet lane, edged with the incredible blue of the wild gentian, she knew she had been right to come. No exhaust fumes, no clatter, no stutter of air hammers tearing up the pavement, no ugly headlines in the paper about riots, no hypocrisy. Only this lovely peace.

They heard the school bus lumbering up the road, and the last hundred yards were covered in a mad dash, with the two biggest boys swinging Andrew between them like a sack of potatoes. They were all flushed and laughing when they stumbled onto the bus, and for just a second, Ellen even forgot to be scared.

But then a wave of sound poored over her, almost drowning her in its volume, and yet she was completely excluded from it. All the kids on the bus were greeting her cousins, yelling the kind of things friends say to each other, insults that aren't real but mean, "You're one of us. You belong."

Only, no one said anything to Ellen. For a minute it looked to her like every seat in the bus was occupied, and she wondered if she would have to stand in the aisle or sit in the back in the midst of what looked like a mass of tangled, shoving boys. She stood rigidly, feeling her cheeks flaming.

Then out of the blur of sound and strange faces, she heard her name being called, and she looked back to see Mary Ann Trevor waving at her.

Gratefully, she pushed past the knot of cousins, who were all looking awkward and uncomfortable, and made her way to where Mary Ann had saved a seat for her.

"Thanks," Ellen said, and dropped down with relief. It had seemed as though everyone was staring at her, and she was grateful to be partially hidden behind the seat in front of her.

"You're welcome," Mary Ann said formally, and they looked cautiously at each other. Down at the dock, leaping in and out of the chill water, everyone screaming and splashing, it had been easy to be relaxed. But here, dressed up and scared, not really knowing any of the kids, Ellen felt more like a stranger than she had ever felt in her life.

For a long minute they were silent, and then Mary Ann said, "You're in ninth grade, aren't you?"

"Yes. Are you?"

"Yes. I hope you're in my room."

Ellen smiled her gratitude. "Oh, me too. I'll die if I don't know anyone."

"The kids are friendly," Mary Ann said. "You won't have any trouble. Too bad you aren't in tenth grade. Then you could have been with your cousin Sam."

Ellen darted a quick look at Mary Ann, and the memory of the boys teasing Sam came back to her. It was possible, of course, that Mary Ann was only being nice because she liked Sam and this was one way to get to see him more often. *Maybe when she finds out Sam doesn't like me and doesn't want me here, she'll stop being friendly,* Ellen thought.

"Sam would probably die if he had to take me with him," Ellen ventured.

Mary Ann only giggled. "Sam's not as awful as he likes to think he is," she said, and there was almost a grown-up sound to her voice.

"Tell me who some of the kids are," Ellen said. "I'll never remember all of them, but tell me anyhow."

Mary Ann pointed out a few, and the names rattled in and out of Ellen's mind like loose pebbles. She felt like she'd never know anyone. Two months from now, she'd probably still not be able to remember a single person except Mary Ann and the four cousins.

"Here we are," Mary Ann said suddenly, and

Ellen looked up to see the beautiful, big, new high school in front of her. She knew this new consolidated school served the entire island, including the Indian reservation on Wikwemikong Peninsula, but she had never seen the inside of it. It would probably be like all other new schools—big and shiny and bright. But it wasn't the building that mattered anyhow. It was the kids who sat near you in classes, the teachers who made the days exciting or dull, the friends or enemies who became a part of your life.

Ellen realized that she was really scared to death, and even Mary Ann's friendliness wasn't helping a bit. Just then she looked up to see Dave staring at her. Very deliberately, and without paying the slightest bit of attention to anyone else who might be watching, he lowered his left eyelid in a wink that said a thousand things. It said, "Don't be scared. You'll be okay. Don't forget you've got us. Everything is going to be great."

The terror began to leave her, and she gratefully winked back. As long as God hadn't seen fit to give her a big brother, she would be forever thankful that at least he had provided a cousin like Dave, who could be counted on when things got rough.

The hours in school passed in fits and starts. The hour in art class flew by like wind. It was really almost unbelievable to Ellen, who loved art more than anything else. First, she discovered, she would have the class twice each week, instead of only once. And second, she fell in love at first glance with Miss Numadabi, the teacher, who was Indian. She was tall, slender, dark, and lovely. Her hair was pulled back severely, which only accentuated the high cheekbones, the black eyes. She did a painting for the class to show them how to try to express themselves, and Ellen watched in delight and envy as the slender, dark fingers flew over the paper, creating a scarlet sky over an amber sea and a blur of white that was, miraculously, unmistakably, the lighthouse on Strawberry Island.

Other classes were less exciting, and Ellen endured them, feeling lost and lonely. She had the same teacher, Mr. Adams, for algebra, English, and homeroom. He was all right, she decided, if anyone who taught algebra could be considered normal.

She lost her way once, and stood simply terrified in a section of the hall that seemed to lead nowhere.

"Lost?" The speaker was an Indian girl who had been in Ellen's homeroom and most of her classes. She had a round, merry face and a wide smile that reminded Ellen vaguely of Clarisse.

Ellen nodded, too scared to say anything intelligent.

The friendly smile widened. "I know just how you feel. First time I was in this school, I got lost a hundred times. My name's Rachael, Rachael Enoss. Here, let me see your schedule."

Rachael, like art class and Mary Ann, had made the difference between a day of misery and a day that was bearable. Late that evening Ellen sat in her room and wrote to her father. As she poured out her news, making everything sound as happy as possible so daddy wouldn't worry, she thought back to Mary Ann's saving her a seat, to Rachael's smiling assistance.

"I think I've made two friends," she wrote. The words looked brave and hopeful on paper. Friends were so terribly important.

Perhaps these thoughts were what made her add a postscript to the letter.

"If you see Clarisse, give her my love," she wrote. She sat staring at the sentence soberly and then scratched out the last four words. After a few minutes, she wrote, "tell her I said Hi!"

It was better that way, she decided, more honest somehow.

4

It was Saturday and the sun was shining! *Oh, wow!* thought Ellen almost before she was fully awake. Dave had promised that if the weather were decent, she could go fishing with him. The first two Saturdays she had been here, it had either rained or Dave had been tied up. But today he was free, and from her window she could see the sun streaking gold across the lawn. *Now if only it isn't too windy,* she thought, and rose up on an elbow so she could see down to the water. Several days they had gone to school in the gray sweep of a northeaster that had whipped the bay to a dangerous frenzy. Knowing that a wind could sweep across these waters even when the sun was shining, she felt real anxiety until she saw that the water was relatively smooth, with only small waves tipped with foam that sparkled in the early sunlight.

Oh, wow! she thought again and swung her feet out of bed. For a minute, hearing no talking in the kitchen, she feared that she might have overslept and been left at home, especially when she saw that a note had been shoved under her door. She grabbed it quickly and read Dave's scrawl:

"Had to run into Little Current on an errand for dad. Should be home before nine. Think Sam will go with us. Dress warm; it's not as summerish as it looks. See you, Dave."

Her watch showed nearly eight-thirty, so she dressed quickly, trying not even to think of the fact that Sam would accompany them. She simply wouldn't let Sam ruin this day, that's all there was to it!

Aunt Betty was in the kitchen, sitting at the small table that looked out over the bay, sipping a cup of coffee. As usual, Ellen's heart skipped a beat at this first morning glimpse of her aunt. The likeness to mom was uncanny. It was easier, in some strange way, to just think of her as mom and not keep being stabbed by the way they looked alike.

"Hi, sleepyhead," Aunt Betty said. "I've been up for hours, and I have a message that says if you're not ready at nine, you'll have to swim to catch up with them."

"Why didn't you wake me?" Ellen asked, pouring some cereal into a bowl and putting some bread in the toaster. "I might have slept till noon."

"Oh, I planned to dust the piano keys if you hadn't shown up by eight-thirty," Aunt Betty said, smiling. "Then I heard you leaping about, so I figured you had Dave's note."

The word *dusting* was the one that jumped out at Ellen. She really hadn't done a thing except dry dishes since she came, and daddy had given her orders.

"Aunt Betty," she began, "should I stay home and dust or something? I haven't done much to help at all, and I do want to."

"I like that!" Aunt Betty said, pretending indignation. "Here I cleaned all day yesterday, and you think the place needs dusting."

Ellen giggled. "I hadn't looked. I just thought—"

"No, honey, I'll tell you something. When I was little, your grandma always cleaned on Saturday and your mother and I had to help. I vowed that I'd never do that to my kids. There's plenty you can do to help. And as soon as you're adjusted, we'll work out a schedule. But not on Saturday. I like holidays, too."

"That's *exactly* the way mom felt," Ellen said with satisfaction. "Oh, Aunt Betty, you're just— you're just like her."

"No. I'm not," Aunt Betty said briskly. "You'll

find out how different. But I think I see Dave pulling into the drive, so you better swallow down that toast and get into a warm jacket. Hurry now."

Ellen gulped her last few bites of breakfast and flew into her room for a hooded jacket and a pair of old gloves, which she shoved deep into her pocket. Sam would laugh when he saw her use them, but she simply couldn't bear to thread live, wiggling night crawlers onto her hook with bare hands. Gloves might be sissy, but they were better than wanting to just lie down and die when you had to bait your hook.

In less than fifteen minutes, they were down at the boat. Sam had filled the motor with gas while Dave was on his errand, and he had the rods all ready in the bow of the boat.

"I'll steer," Dave said.

"You did last time," Sam retorted. "I'm sick of being treated like a baby. It's my turn."

Dave shrugged. "Okay, so steer. Only don't play games."

Sam dragged on the starter rope, jolting the motor into roaring life with such a suddenness that Ellen, stepping into the boat, nearly lost her balance. Dave grabbed her arm, and in a second she was seated safely in the seat nearest the bow. Dave sat in the middle, and Sam was back at the stern, handling the outboard.

"What's the matter?" Sam laughed. "Afraid I

might scare our little Yankee cousin?"

They all called her Yankee sometimes, but from the rest of them it had a ring of affection. From Sam it sounded insulting. Ellen felt a sudden anger burn in her throat, and she wanted to say something nasty in reply. But to say anything against his use of the word would almost make it necessary to say something equally insulting about Canada, and that was ridiculous. She was here because this was the country she wanted to be in—this free, large, lovely place. So she just ignored the taunt.

"I don't know about her," Dave said calmly. "But you could scare *me* if you get to acting too much like a cowboy."

"Chicken," Sam sneered, and they roared away from the dock, missing the pilings by inches and creating a wake that splashed against the shore so loudly that Ellen got a glimpse of Aunt Betty running to the door to look out.

"You know the rules," Dave said, lifting his voice to be heard above the motor. "No more than three miles per hour until you're well away from shore. Shape up!"

Sam said something in reply that Ellen couldn't hear, but his face looked red and angry. Sam idolized Dave, even when he was doing all the things that irritated his older brother, so no doubt he was humiliated at being yelled at in front of her. She wished terribly that she could do something to make the two boys look less angry, but she could only sit helplessly, feeling the boat rock beneath her as Sam turned the motor to full speed.

It wasn't a large motor—only a 40 H.P.—but the boat was just a light aluminum shell, and it tore over the water at what seemed like an incredible speed. All at once, the bumpiness ceased, and it was almost as though they were flying, with the wind sharp in her face.

"What smoothed it out?" she yelled at Dave.

"We're planing," he yelled back. "The boat goes so fast it skims on top of the water instead of plowing through it. But this isn't the place to do it. There are some rocks in this channel."

He turned to Sam. "Cut it back!" he yelled, and Ellen could hear the words because Dave was really shouting. "Cut it back till we get out in the deep water."

Sullenly, Sam pulled back on the throttle and the boat slowed down.

They rode in silence, both boys avoiding looking at the other, and Ellen felt intensely uncomfortable. But she simply didn't know what to do or say, so she half turned in her seat to watch the scenery going by.

In spite of the tension, she could feel something almost like a joyful ache. *Who could stay upset or angry with this around them?* she thought. The water stretched north and west of them as far as the eye could see, interrupted only by the green islands that thrust up everywhere.

The wake of the boat sparkled and flowed behind them in a long, curving line of loveliness, and Ellen gazed back along the side of the boat, trying to see it all, trying to memorize how it looked so she could remember on a dark winter day.

"Am I allowed to go faster now, sir?" Sam asked with mock humility.

"Knock it off," Dave said gruffly. For a second, Ellen saw them glare at each other, and then a grin touched Dave's mouth and Sam relented with an answering grin.

"Would you be scared?" Sam yelled at Ellen.

"No," she yelled back. "I like it when you plane."

Sam looked surprised. "Here we go," he shouted, and the next twenty minutes were like flying and dipping back onto the water and flying again, and the water splashed her face with a chill excitement.

They finally pulled up close to one of the little islands, and Ellen sat in silence while the boys maneuvered the boat, selecting the exact place to drop anchor. They argued as though a single foot away from the right spot could matter.

"How can you be so sure of the right place?" Ellen asked at last. "It all looks alike to me."

"Well, it doesn't to a bass," Sam said.

"He's right," Dave agreed, and she knew that their anger was at least cooled for now, for which she was grateful. It would be just too awful to have the whole day ruined.

"Here, Sam, right here," Dave said positively, and the anchor hit the water with a splash.

In a few minutes, the boat swung gently into the wind, and they rocked quietly in the sudden silence that surrounded them as the motor was shut off.

Ellen handed out the rods, and Sam got the carton of night crawlers out from under his seat.

"I suppose we'll have to bait your hook," he said to Ellen.

It really took all her courage to answer him. "I have old gloves," she said. "So I won't have to touch them."

Sam looked honestly astonished and disgusted. "City people sure are weird," he said. "Gloves, for the love of pete!"

"I'll bait your hook if you want," Dave said.

"No, I'll do it. It's—it's just that they wiggle, and I feel like I'm hurting them," Ellen confessed, looking only at Dave.

For some reason Sam didn't laugh at this, as she had expected. Without additional comment, Dave handed her a dark red worm, which she took gingerly in her gloved fingers.

It took her quite a few minutes to thread the wriggling thing onto the hook, leaving the loops as Dave had taught her two years ago. Several times she nearly gave in and asked Dave to help, but she grimly stuck to it, trying not to wince too much, and when she was finished, she looked up in triumph.

Both boys were watching her, and she was surprised to see admiration on both faces.

"Good," said Dave briefly. "Now, you try over that side. Do you remember how to let it down till the weight touches the bottom and then reel up one or two turns?"

She nodded and dropped the worm into the water.

"Not bad for a city gal—and a Yankee to boot," Sam said.

"Maybe I'm part Ludlow," she shot back at him, and he cast his eyes to heaven and groaned in dismay.

But this kind of banter she could take. It was the real anger and irritation that he showed at times that hurt. *Maybe,* she thought, but just then her thoughts were shattered by a quick, hard tug on her line.

"That's no rock bass," she gasped to Dave.

"Don't think so," he said. "Keep the tip up. Keep it *up*."

The line was spinning out and the reel handle banged her knuckle cruelly as she fought to keep the rod steady. She had never had anything like this on her line before. But, then, she had never fished in late September before either, and they had always told her that fishing got better as the weather got cooler and the tourists got fewer.

"You've really got something," Sam said. "For

crying out loud, don't be dumb and lose it. Give him some line."

She tried turning the handle of her reel, and Sam's voice came sharp and harsh. "Don't reel it in, stupid. Give him line!"

She was beginning to feel panic churn in her, and her crazy instinct was to fire the rod at Sam's head and yell, "Give him line yourself if you're so smart."

But then Dave's voice came soothingly. "Let the reel spin, Ellen. You've hooked something big. Let him run with the line."

"Help me," she begged. "I don't know what to do."

"Take the rod, Dave," Sam said. "Don't trust her with it."

"Shut up, Sam," Dave said. "Come on, Ellen, you can do it. Look, see, he's slowing. Now reel. Reel fast. Keep the line taut. Thatta girl. No— now, wait—he's going again. Let the reel spin."

It took five minutes that seemed like five hours, but with Dave's coaching and her own terrible need to land this fish and show Sam she wasn't so stupid after all, Ellen brought the fish to the edge of the boat.

"A beauty," Dave said. "We'll have to net him. Here, Sam hold my rod."

"She'll lose it," Sam warned mournfully.

"No, she won't. Come on, Ellen, lead him into this net. Slow. Easy. Don't let him touch the boat or he'll knock himself loose. Okay, now, easy does it—easy—there! We've got him!"

The net seemed bulging with the thrashing dark bass, and Ellen found that her arms were suddenly trembling so hard she could hardly hold onto her rod.

"I got him," she bragged to anyone who would listen. "I got him."

It turned out that the fish weighed three and one-half pounds when they got it unhooked and weighed.

"Talk about beginner's luck," Sam said, but he was grinning.

"This'll be something to write home about," Dave said.

Ellen watched him put the fish on a stringer, and she felt that this was true happiness—this minute in the sunshine with the fish brought safely in.

They fished for several more hours, and the boys caught some nice bass, but nothing to equal Ellen's. She fished, too, but not with any real enthusiasm. To want more seemed almost like being greedy. Besides, it seemed like "her" fish was the biggest and most beautiful thing these waters had to offer, and she was content to just sit and feel the sun on her head and shoulders and watch the boys.

At noon they pulled anchor and went around the little island to a miniature bay on the other side, where it was easy to bring the light boat up to the shore. They climbed out onto the land. Dave brought out the box of lunch Aunt Betty had packed. There was good Canadian cheese, some late tomatoes, hard-boiled eggs, buttered homemade bread, cookies, and cans of cold pop in the foam-insulated box. Ellen felt that she had never in her entire life tasted anything so good.

They heard the motor of another boat, sounding nearer than it was, due to the odd way sound travels over water. As the boat got nearer, Dave shaded his eyes against the sun. "Looks like the Enoss boys," he said at last.

Sam stood on the shore and waved. The boys in the approaching boat returned the wave, and in a few minutes they had pulled into the tiny bay.

"Come on and sit down awhile," Dave said. "There's some pop left, I think. And maybe cookies."

"Sure." The boys pulled their boat up onto shore and stepped out. Ellen looked with some curiosity to see if they moved in the lithe, silent way that she had always associated with Indians, but they walked like any boy she had ever seen, and Freddie, in fact, stumbled on a rock and said a short, hard word that she didn't quite catch.

"Let's take a walk," Sam said to Freddie, and the two of them set off around the shore of the little island, jumping from stone to stone, laughing and talking, and the sound of their voices drifted back like an echo.

Tom and Dave started to talk about fishing and football and other ordinary things that boys talk about, and Ellen just sat and listened. It was good talk, easy talk. There was no mention made of the fact that Dave lived on the north shore of the island and Tom came from the eastern peninsula where Wikwemikong was located. It seemed to her, there in the pine-scented sunshine, that there was absolutely no difference between the boys. The fact that Dave had blue eyes, fair skin, and light brown hair and that Tom had black eyes and hair, high prominent cheekbones, and dark skin were as unimportant as the fact that Tom wore blue jeans and Dave wore tan chinos.

Oh, this is the way it should be, Ellen thought. *This is the way I want it to be. I was right about the island. Clarisse and I could be friends here and no one would care.*

The other two boys returned from their circuit of the island, and Sam was holding a small bird in his hands. For one heart-sinking minute Ellen thought he had captured it and was going to hurt it.

But when he spoke, his voice was oddly gentle for Sam. "Little fellow has a broken wing," he said. "I'll take him home and set it. Come on, Dave. I promised mom we wouldn't stay too long, so she wouldn't worry."

Ellen stared at him with her mouth open. This was a side of Sam she had never suspected.

Sam looked at her and the gentleness was gone

as he snapped, "Don't gawk at me. Get in the boat and see if you can sit still on the way home."

Dave opened his mouth to speak, but Ellen shot him a beseeching look. Let it go, she implored silently. Don't make it any more embarrassing than it is.

Dave seemed to understand and only said, "I'm steering going home."

Sam made no protest but sat in the middle seat, his back to Ellen and his hands cupped protectively about the small bird.

Ellen got into the boat, and Dave shoved off smoothly. The Enoss boys followed them from the shore and then headed in a different direction, waving a casual farewell.

The motor started up and Ellen sat in silence looking at Sam's back. She was so totally confused that her mind was whirling. She simply couldn't figure out what made him act as he did—pleasant one minute and rude the next. Her prayer that Sam might turn into a friend seemed no closer to being answered than it had the first night she came.

In spite of Sam, though, the day had been completely beautiful, enough for a year. Maybe even for a lifetime.

5

The weeks moved swiftly past and by late October Ellen was beginning to feel that all of the major adjustments had been made. There was no letup in the feud between her and Sam, but there had not been any open warfare either. By turn he was moody, rude, and tolerant. She simply had no idea why he acted at he did, and it really bothered her at times. She wondered if she could possibly make her permanent home in a house where one of the members seemed to dislike her so much. She realized now that it had been different when Randy and Clarisse quarreled. They had a basic affection for each other, and the quarrels had just flared up and died down. Sam really seemed at times to be an enemy, and this fact kept her feeling like a visitor in a house where she wanted to feel like family.

The rest of the Ludlows were wonderful. Uncle Archie and Aunt Betty treated her exactly as though she belonged to them, even to the point of scolding her if she left her jacket in the living room or spent too much time in front of the tv on school nights. She reminded herself of this when she got depressed over Sam. *Visitors don't get scolded,* she told herself, *only family.*

The really important thing was school. After all, that was where she spent the larger part of her time. Mary Ann Trevor continued to save a seat for her every morning on the bus; and although Ellen appreciated it, she still wasn't sure whether it was because of herself or Sam.

Then one day that little problem ironed itself out in such a natural way that Ellen felt ashamed of her early suspicions. It was a Friday, and Mary Ann grinned at her as Ellen dropped into the seat beside her on the bus.

"Friday, thank heavens," Mary Ann said. "I really don't think I could bear another day of algebra. I may just have to kill myself it's so awful."

"I know," Ellen said sympathetically. "I'd join you in a suicide pact, except I have Dave to help me when it gets too grim."

"How about Sam?" Mary Ann said casually. "He had it only last year, and to hear him tell it, he's a genius."

Ellen hesitated and then decided to take the plunge. If it turned Mary Ann off, well, then she was sorry. "Sam can't stand me," she confided. "I think he really hates it that I'm living there."

Mary Ann grinned at her. "Sam used to hate me, too," she said. "He's weird. But nice when you get to know him well enough to forget the weirdness."

"It's different with you," Ellen blurted out. "I'm his cousin."

Surprisingly enough, Mary Ann agreed with her. "Yeah, you're right there. But you wait, something will happen that will make him know that you're not—well, someone to be afraid of."

"Afraid of?" Ellen felt her voice scale up in amazement. She looked around quickly to see if anyone was listening. "He isn't afraid of anything."

Mary Ann shook her head. "He's afraid of practically everything. That's why he acts so tough. You wait, he'll find out you're nice soon enough."

Ellen looked into Mary Ann's hazel eyes and saw only kindness there.

"Do you think I'm nice?" she asked awkwardly, but she had to know.

Mary Ann looked shy. "I think you're the nicest girl in my class," she said. "It's been so neat having a girl next door. I'd come over a lot more, only Sam might think—he might think—"

"I know," Ellen giggled, relief filling her with a

sort of giddiness, "that you can't resist his charm."

Mary Ann giggled, too, and in that minute Ellen knew she had a friend.

"You can come to my place anytime, though," Mary Ann said. "That way, it'll be okay."

Ellen had been right that first day of school. The other girl who was her friend was Rachael. She was very short, a little plump, and her black eyes had a slight slant to them that gave her an almost Oriental look. She wore her heavy black hair in a fringe of bangs across her forehead and hanging straight to her shoulders. She dressed neatly and attractively, and her smile was as bright as sunshine.

Some of the Indian kids dressed pretty sloppily, Ellen had to concede, but then, so did some of the white kids. It was just like home. Clarisse, for example, had been one of the best dressed girls in school, and her modified Afro had been perfect for her slender oval face. But some of the black kids had looked like weirdos, and there had been even more white kids who looked really freaked out. So Rachael's attractiveness did not seem unusual to Ellen; it was only part of what Rachael was.

They sat beside each other in several classes, and the more they got to know each other, the better Ellen liked her. They discovered that they both adored art and Miss Numadabi, and they both loathed algebra and thought Mr. Adams was neat even if his English assignments were totally unfair because they were so long.

It was in art class that they got to know each other best. They seemed to feel exactly alike about the joy of trying to paint.

One day, after art class, Rachael turned rather abruptly to Ellen as they came through the door.

"Would you like to come to my house?" she said in a quick voice.

"I'd love to," Ellen said promptly. She had hoped that Rachael would ask her, because she had never been on any reservation and she wanted very much to go. "But how could I? That's pretty far to ask Uncle Archie to drive me."

"You could go home with me Friday on the school bus," Rachael said. "There's always at least one empty seat, and we could get permission at the office. Maybe your uncle or Dave could come for you after supper."

"Oh, that would be really great," Ellen said. "I'd like that. I'll ask Aunt Betty tonight, and if she says okay and someone can come after me, I'd really love it. You'll have to tell me where you live."

Rachael's explanation was illustrated by a small map she drew, leaning against one of the walls in the hall. "Here," she said, "your uncle or Dave could follow this. Ours is the newly painted house."

"I'll ask," Ellen promised, "and let you know in homeroom tomorrow."

Rachael grinned. "I'm glad you want to come."

"Well, of course, I *want* to," Ellen said and ran to her next class, almost colliding with one of the big boys in the hall.

That night, at the supper table, Ellen brought up the subject of Rachael's invitation. There was an immediate flash of interchanged looks around the table, and Ellen wasn't sure whether they were pleased looks because she was beginning to make friends, or if there was a questioning look on the part of Uncle Archie and Aunt Betty. It was impossible, she felt, that there would be any problem over the fact that Rachael was an Indian. Look at the way the boys had acted that day they went fishing. Maybe her aunt and uncle didn't know the Enoss family; of course, if they didn't, they would want to be sure they were nice people. That much she knew without question. Adults were ridiculously fussy about things like this, and Daddy always acted like he'd feel better if a private detective could sleuth out anyone Ellen knew before he'd trust his precious child with them.

"Rachael is really nice," Ellen added quickly, "and Dave and Sam know her brothers."

Uncle Archie's glance went swiftly to Dave and Sam.

To Ellen's surprise, Sam spoke up first. "Freddie's a good guy. I've never been at his house, but he's a good guy, if that means anything."

Now, what in the world does a remark like that

mean? Ellen thought in exasperation.

"They're nice people," Dave said. "I know Tom pretty well, I mean, better than most guys. They've been talking about moving away from the reservation, Tom says. Their dad has a pretty good job."

The old private detection business is as active in Canada as in the U.S., Ellen thought in disgust. *For crying out loud, I'm not interested in Mr. Enoss's job or where or how they live. I only want to visit Rachael.*

"Rachael's great," she repeated. "She certainly is friendlier than Karen Richardson, and they live in one of the biggest houses in Little Current."

"Amen!" said Dave fervently, and Ellen was uncomfortably aware of an undercurrent of sarcasm in Dave's voice, which was unusual. Maybe she hadn't been wise in using Karen as a comparison. Uncle Archie and Mr. Richardson were pretty friendly, she knew.

"Well, I just think we can't be too careful," Aunt Betty murmured, and for the first time Ellen felt irritated with her aunt, wondering if, like most adults, she had ridiculous rules and standards that were too rigid to be intelligent.

"You don't have to worry, mom," Dave said. "They have a clean house, Rachael is a good little kid, and Mrs. Enoss hangs out a white wash!"

The sarcasm in the last few words was plain enough to be felt, and it made Ellen feel jumpy inside. Dave wasn't usually like this. Something about this whole conversation was getting inside him, and not in a pleasant way.

"I'm sorry," Ellen faltered. "I don't mean to cause trouble. If you don't want me to go, Aunt Betty, or if it's too much trouble to pick me up, why then, okay."

But the tremble in her voice was a strange mixture of concern over Dave and a vague, troubled anger. It was all so silly—the whole thing. She had only asked to go to visit a girl, and they were going on like she was planning to take a trip to the moon.

"I can go after her," Dave offered. "I want to go out for awhile Friday night, anyhow, and Dad already said I could have the car. I won't be late. I can pick her up about nine or so."

Aunt Betty hesitated, and once more she and Uncle Archie looked at each other. What was there about adults when they looked at each other like that? It was as though they had each said a dozen sentences and the other one knew just what had been said. It was spooky.

"I think it might be all right," Aunt Betty said. "You're sure you don't mind going after her?" The last remark was directed at Dave.

"I don't want to cause any trouble," Ellen said again.

"No trouble." Dave was very matter of fact. "I'm going to be driving through Manitowaning anyway, so I can go over by the reservation and pick you up. No trouble."

Aunt Betty looked like she wanted to say more, but she just smiled—only it wasn't her usual warm smile—and said to Ellen, "Okay, honey, you tell Rachael you can come. I hope you have a lovely time."

"Oh, thanks," Ellen said, but she didn't feel as relaxed about it as she wanted to. They had just made such a big deal about the whole thing. "I've never been to the reservation. I think it ought to be fun."

"They eat roast rattlesnake for dinner," Sam warned with a malicious grin.

Phillip was the one to refute that even before Ellen could open her mouth. "There aren't any rattlesnakes on this whole island, so how could they eat them? That's dumb. They'll probably have baked ham or something ordinary like that."

Ellen shuddered, then she spoke tartly to Sam. "I'll tell Freddie you suggested it. Maybe he'll hire you to go looking for one."

Sam glared at her. "Don't bother telling Freddie *anything*."

It was strange how clearly Ellen got his message. He really didn't want her to repeat his senseless remark to Freddie, because it was insulting and stupid, and Sam didn't want Freddie to know he had been guilty of such dumbness. For the first time since she came to the island, Ellen had a small weapon to hold over Sam's head.

So she didn't answer him at all. She only smiled a small, secret smile and had the satisfaction of knowing that he was uncomfortable and unhappy and that he wished he had held his tongue.

The ride to the reservation Friday evening was awkward, but no more awkward than any bus ride with a large group of kids who knew each other very well but to whom Ellen was a total stranger. Some of them stared at Ellen and Rachael, some of them ignored the two girls, but no one was either openly rude or friendly. There was only one girl whose smile at Rachael was warm enough to include Ellen. She was a lovely girl—very slender with long, straight black hair, large black eyes, and features that were even and pretty. She moved as though she were dancing, Ellen thought. No, that wasn't the word. But she was so graceful that she made every other girl on the bus look awkward. Ellen had seen her several times in the hall at school or in the art room, and every time she had wondered about her, simply because she was so attractive, really almost beautiful.

"Who's she?" Ellen whispered to Rachael.

"Debbie Wawaskesh," Rachael answered. "She's in the same grade as your cousin Dave. She wants to go to the university, but her grandfather—"

"Are her parents dead?" Ellen asked, feeling an

instant sympathy toward the lovely Debbie. She *knew* how that was—even halfway.

"I guess so. Or they left the island or something. Anyhow, Debbie lives with her grandfather, old Pete Wawaskesh. He's really neat. He still believes in old-time Indian stuff."

Ellen looked at Rachael in amazement. She was talking as though she weren't even an Indian herself.

"Don't *you*?" she asked.

Rachael laughed. "Of course not. I'm Christian—we go to church just like you do. My folks gave up on the old superstitions long ago. Oh, we take part in the powwow every year and stuff like that. But we don't pay any attention to the moon and stones and animals the way Pete does." She giggled. "He'd probably just as soon go back and live in the wilderness like Indians used to. Maybe he would if it weren't for Debbie."

"Then—then, you don't—well, live any different?" Ellen asked, saying the words cautiously so she wouldn't hurt Rachael's feelings.

But Rachael was very hearty. "We don't, not at my house. Of course, my dad works hard. The Indian Affairs people sent him away from home while he was still a little boy—they didn't even ask his parents' permission—so he's educated and has a good job. And my mother is awful fussy. That's why, well, we'd like to move off the reservation. Some of the people there, some of them are lazy, my dad says, and live off the government."

"Like our welfare people," Ellen said, nodding in understanding. "I guess there are always people who are like that."

Rachael gazed at her with something like awe. "You don't seem at all surprised that we aren't all alike on the reservation," she said in astonishment. "Most people—"

But her sentence was cut off by the abrupt stopping of the bus, and the girls discovered that they had reached their destination. They got off in a flurry of kids yelling good-byes. In all the confusion, Ellen managed to get one last glimpse of Debbie, smiling at her with a sweetness that was both delightful and surprising. She wondered fleetingly why Debbie, so much older, would bother being so friendly to a kid like her, and a stranger at that.

The evening at the Enoss home was pleasant. It was not really comfortable, because Ellen was still a stranger, but it was exciting because everything was new and each impression was sharply etched on her mind. Mr. and Mrs. Enoss were friendly but quiet, neither of them much like the warm Rachael or the boisterous Freddie or even the confident Tom. But they made Ellen feel at home, particularly when Mr. Enoss bowed his head at the beginning of the meal. She had become so used to the casual way the Ludlows started eating without saying grace that she had almost started to pick up her fork. Fortunately, she was watching Rachael's father, so she had time to drop her hands to her lap.

"Thank you, Father," Mr. Enoss said, "for the work of the day, for this food and this fellowship. Amen."

"Amen," Ellen murmured and looked up to see Rachael watching her. They smiled and then turned their attention to the food.

It wasn't ham at all, but some delicious concoction of fish and rice, and the bread was homemade and still warm from the oven. Ellen ate until she was stuffed, and Mrs. Enoss beamed at her.

"I just can't eat another bite," Ellen said, eyeing the second piece of moist chocolate cake that Mrs. Enoss was trying to press on her. "I'd blow up and burst."

"That's a better way of getting rid of a paleface than scalping him," Freddie observed, but his father eyed him with such sternness that his cocky grin disappeared in a blur of embarrassment.

Mrs. Enoss said something sharply, words that Ellen could not understand, and it was a jolt to her that these people actually *did* speak a different language. She had known lots of kids in Pittsburgh and later in Washington who came from homes where Italian, Hungarian, or Spanish was spoken. But somehow these strange syllables had such an ancient sound to them that they made little shivers run across her arms.

After dinner the girls did dishes together and then went to Rachael's room and played records and talked and tried to imagine what it would be like if Miss Numadabi would choose them to represent the ninth graders in the art show in the spring. Debbie Wawaskesh was really the best art student in school, Rachael said. She acted as a sort of assistant to Miss Numadabi, and she sometimes helped the younger kids.

"She's helped me a lot," Rachael said. "I'll ask her to help you, too, if you want."

"That would be wonderful," Ellen said. "I'd love that!"

After a few seconds, Rachael, said, "Ellen, can I ask you something? You said 'Amen' when my father prayed. Does that mean you, well, really believe? Not just go to church, I mean, but believe for yourself?"

Ellen answered slowly, "I don't go to church much up here. Aunt Betty does and Andrew goes to Sunday school, but Uncle Archie and the other boys don't, and I've started sleeping in. I've, well, sort of lost faith in churches; but I do believe in God, if that's what you mean."

Rachael only smiled sympathetically, and Ellen stumbled on. "It was nice to be in a house again where someone says grace. My father would have a stroke if we started eating without prayer."

Rachael giggled. "Mine, too. He often tells us

that when we say grace we can be all Indian, and all Christian. Thanking God for food is normal for Indians."

"I guess it ought to be normal for everybody," Ellen murmured, warm in the realization that she had found someone with whom she could talk about something like this.

And I didn't find her in church, she thought defiantly.

The whole evening was so pleasant that Ellen really hated to see nine o'clock come, but Dave arrived almost promptly on the hour. He refused to come in, saying that he had a long way to drive and he had promised his mother they wouldn't be late.

"You'll come again, won't you?" Rachael pleaded. "They'll let you come again?"

"As long as it isn't too much trouble to get me," Ellen said.

Tom, who had been lounging in front of the tv, looked up and grinned. "Don't think Dave will mind coming down. Will you, Dave?"

For some peculiar reason, Dave lost his usually serene look and grinned with somethng that was a curious mixture of embarrassment and good humor. "It's a nice drive," was all he said, but he and Tom were communicating on a level that did not include anyone else in the room.

"And you can come to my place, too," Ellen said to Rachael. "Can't she, Dave?"

"Don't see why not," Dave agreed. "Maybe even

stay all night. Isn't that what girls like to do? Giggle till all hours?"

Ellen and Rachael giggled, as if his words had been a cue in a play, and they exchanged looks of pleasure.

"Thank you, Mrs. Enoss," Ellen said politely, remembering her training. "I had a wonderful time."

"Then come again," Mrs. Enoss said. "Anytime."

Dave and Ellen were quiet for the first few miles, but Ellen was very much aware of the boy beside her. There was something strange about Dave tonight—something different, as if he were excited or terribly happy or all keyed up about something. She couldn't imagine what it might be. At home, a boy this different from his usual calm behavior would arouse instant suspicions in her mind that he might have been smoking pot. But the idea of Dave smoking pot was as silly as the idea of Uncle Archie walking down the main street in Little Current without any clothes on. Dave didn't even smoke ordinary cigarettes, and he said beer tasted like soap. No, whatever it was that had Dave so high was nothing that could be swallowed or inhaled.

She finally spoke into the quiet. "You seem happy. Did something nice happen?"

Dave shot a quick look at her. "Yeah. I heard we

won the first basketball game of the season."

"Oh, come on," Ellen said. "Don't put me on."

"Would you believe I caught a twelve-foot bass out of Manitou Lake?"

"Sure. From the shore. With no rod."

"Okay. No game, no bass, and a little cousin who is too young to know everything in the world."

"I like that!" she said indignantly. "If it's something that's none of my business, say so. But don't tell me I'm too young."

"Sorry," he said. "That's a lousy thing to say. I guess I wouldn't—couldn't—even tell you if you were older. But, I'll tell you this much. When I can tell anyone—anyone at all—you'll be the first one I'll tell. Okay?"

And she had to be content with that. But after a long silence, she said, "I had a gorgeous time tonight."

He grinned at her briefly. "So did I, little cousin. So did I!"

6

There had been a heavy frost in the night and even a light skim of snow that melted off in the Saturday sunshine. But the wind blew with a bite, and Ellen could smell the coming winter. She went down the lane after the mail and walked slowly back, reading a letter from her father, warming herself with his love and concern. She felt only the tiniest smidge of guilt at his usual reminder to pray each night. True, her prayers had been reduced almost to the "God blesses" of her little girlhood, but since God hadn't done anything about making Sam nicer so that she could like him, she had decided to quit asking. Sometimes she tried to justify it by deciding that Sam wasn't supposed to be her friend. Most of the time, she pushed the whole thing out of her mind, just as she had pushed it out of her prayers.

She started across the yard and looked down toward the dock. Sam and Andrew were fooling around with the boat, although she had heard Uncle Archie say last night that today was the day to get the motor off and into the shed and the boat onto land. Sam was surely too light to handle that motor, she mused, and Andy would be only a nuisance. She wondered what they were doing.

Just then Andrew looked up and saw her.

"Hey, Ellen," he shouted, his little-boy grin lighting up his face. "We're going for one last ride before Dave and dad take the boat in. Want to come?"

She could see Sam saying something to Andrew, but the words were indistinguishable. She knew what he must be saying, though. Of course, he wouldn't want her to come. And she wasn't at all sure that she wanted to go. The water looked cold, even with the sun turning it deep blue, and the wind would be bitter out on the lake.

Andrew was arguing with Sam. His shrill voice carried clearly.

"I *want* her to go," he said. "Phil and Dave got out this morning, and now the rest of us can have a turn."

Again Sam muttered something, and once more

Andy's voice came clearly. "She is *too* one of the family. And I want her to go."

Ellen was torn between a great reluctance to go when Sam so obviously didn't want her, and a real longing to have one last ride before the boat was permanently beached.

Sam shrugged and said something that must have been reluctant agreement—for all his roughness, he was always curiously kind to Andy, wrestling and teasing sometimes, but never mean—because the little boy turned to his cousin with delight.

"Come on, he says you can go," he shouted.

Her pride held her still for another long minute, and then Ellen thought, *Why not? It's going to be a long winter.* She ran down the slope to the dock, slipping once and almost falling in a shady place where the sun had not yet melted the frost.

"Sure you don't mind, Sam?" she asked, deliberately making her voice friendly.

"Couldn't care less," he said. "One more person won't make any difference."

She started to climb in and Sam looked at her with a superior smile. "Don't come unless you're sure you can take it. I'm going to really let 'er out!"

Andrew squealed with eager anticipation. "Let 'er out all the way, Sam," he yelled. "Make 'er go as fast as lightning!"

"Better wait till you're far enough from the dock so that you don't get your father on your back," was all Ellen said, although she felt a strange little jump in her chest. It *had* been fun going fast—the wind in her face that day they went fishing had been exciting—but that day the water had been calmer, the wind had been sweet and cool, not strong and cold, and Dave had been in the boat, a safety against danger. But she would rather die than let Sam know she was the least bit afraid.

"I'm not scared of anyone on *my* back," Sam boasted, with a look more suitable to Andy's age than to his own.

He jerked the starting rope with the same wild abandon he had used before, and the motor caught with a sudden loud roar. Ellen knew enough about boats now to know that he should immediately throttle back to avoid stalling, or avoid a dangerously fast start away from the dock if the motor didn't stall. But Sam didn't throttle back, and the motor did not stall. They went away from the dock at a crazy angle that slid Andrew along the middle seat like a small pile of light cork. Ellen grabbed him, but he only laughed at her, struggling to be free.

"I'm okay. I like the way Sam makes it go."

There was a sort of dull *ping* as the boat grazed on of the pilings, and Ellen could not avoid looking quickly at Sam for confirmation. Had they hurt the boat?

"Aluminum can take anything," Sam yelled above the sound of the motor. "It only touched us.

And I know every rock in this channel, so don't act like a girl. Unless you want to go back," he offered as an afterthought.

Ellen was filled with the strangest feeling that she ought to say, *Yes, I want to go back. I want all of us to go back. This isn't any fun and it could be dangerous.* But Sam would really make fun of her if she did, and besides, she'd never be able to persuade Andy to go back on land with her. And if it was going to be dangerous, Andrew, light and small and heedless of the threat of the water, needed someone to look after him. Sam loved Andy—anyone could see that—but it was more important to Sam that he show off than to really look after Andrew. No, the best place for her, whether or not she liked it, was right here in the wildly careening boat, gripping the seat with both hands and watching Andy every minute.

She didn't want Sam to see her fear. She knew, somehow, that if he could see her fear, he would only do something more dangerous. So she tried valiantly to pretend that she was having fun.

"Can you make it plane?" she yelled above the noise of motor and wind.

"Too rough," Sam yelled back briefly, and she could see that his knuckles were white as he fought the tiller.

Then why don't you slow down? she wanted to rage at him, but she was afraid to risk it.

Andrew had been laughing with delight. But as

the cold got more intense when they went away from the shore and the wind came sweeping across the water, he began to shiver violently, and Ellen saw the tears in his eyes. Not weepy tears, but the kind that are caused by wind.

"Don't you think we ought to take it a little easier?" Ellen yelled then. "It's really rough and cold."

"See, Andy?" Sam said, shouting so Ellen could hear him. "I told you Yankees were scaredy-cats. Shall we show her how a real Canadian rides a boat?"

Andrew slid his eyes toward Ellen, and there was a struggle in them.

"What do you say, Andy? Canadian style?" Sam shouted.

Canadian style, Ellen thought with real scorn. *Were there ever two more staunch Canadian boys than Dave and Phil? Or a man wiser or braver than Uncle Archie? But none of them ran a boat like this. They went fast only when conditions were right for it—when the water was calmer, when they were sure of the depth, when everyone in the boat was safely seated and relaxed.* But she kept quiet, although she felt something like pity in her heart as she watched Andy's little head bob an agreement to Sam.

Poor little guy. Of course, he had to agree. Sam had already pushed the throttle almost completely open, and now he shoved it the remaining half inch and began zigzagging across the waves so that the boat bobbed like a cork, dipping sideways with sickening lurches as the waves came in at a wrong angle to the boat.

Ellen watched with growing fear at the way Andrew slid and bounced on the seat. He was on the long middle seat, and there was nothing for him to hang onto unless he would grip the seat on either side of him, but he must have felt this would mark him as a sissy. She saw the sudden fear in his eyes and opened her mouth to yell at Sam, to risk everything on a shouted demand for sensible responsibility. Act your age, she was going to say.

But she had waited just a fraction too long. A wave, steeper than the others, struck the boat almost broadside. Sam was making no attempt at all to quarter the waves, to hit them so that there would be the least danger of capsizing. For a terrifying minute, the boat stood almost on its side, water pouring in over the low side, and the huge wave tall enough to splash in over the uptilted side.

Ellen, in the bow, was hanging on so tightly that she remained safely in her seat; and Sam, struggling with the motor, had the tiller to hold, to keep him in the boat. But Andy, trying so hard to be brave, to impress his big brother, had no handhold at all, and he slid out of the boat into the angry water too swiftly for Ellen to loosen a hand to grab him.

The wind tore her scream out of her mouth and ripped it to shreds like a whisper. The look of horror on Sam's face met her own wild gaze as, fighting fiercely, he managed to right the boat.

They both knew that Andrew could swim like a fish, and it didn't appear that he had hit his head in going over. But they also knew that the water was bitterly cold and that it could shock the little boy into possible unconsciousness. Furthermore, he was wearing heavy clothes that would drag him down.

Ellen unzipped her parka in an instant and kicked off her heavy shoes in less time than she had ever dreamed possible. Sam had throttled the boat to a whisper.

"If she stalls, we might swamp," Sam said in a knotted, scared voice. "Where *is* he?"

"There," Ellen said. She was standing, hanging grimly onto one edge. "Right back of you I can just see him under the water. Let me go over the edge, but hang onto my hair so you don't lose us both. I can get him and you can lift us in."

They didn't argue over the silly futile idea of who should go in after Andrew. Sam had to handle the boat; there was only Ellen.

O dear God, she prayed, more frightened than she had ever been in her life. *Help me. Please help me!* The water looked steel gray instead of blue, and she knew that she couldn't really tell how deep down Andrew was. The clear water was deceiving.

"Let yourself over the edge easy," Sam said. "He's just under the surface. Air in his clothes is making him float. Here, I'll hold your hair. Don't jump or the shock will knock you out, too."

The boat was rocking beneath her, and she wondered if she could do it. But, even as she wondered, she slid off the side of the boat into the shockingly cold water. It was worse than cold. It was like pain shooting through her body, and she cried out involuntarily. *I can't move,* she thought in despair. *I'm frozen stiff.*

But then her hands and arms began to move and with Sam's hands steering her head—she never even felt her hair pull—she found herself over the spot where Andy was. He was deeper than they thought, and Sam had to let go of her hair and let her go down—push her down with his hand on top of her head. When the icy water closed over her face, she thought she was dying, but then her foot touched the little boy, and new strength, born of hope, let her bend, reach, and grab, and then the sweet, solid feel of him was in in her hands. She struck for the surface, experiencing a sudden new fear that she'd come up under the lurching boat. But Sam's hand was there, grabbing first her head and then her arm, and pulling her to the edge of the boat. He held the tiller with his knee while he wrestled Andrew out of her arms and up over the edge. He flopped the little boy down on his stomach on the bottom of the boat and then stretched over for Ellen.

Her strength was suddenly gone. Her legs felt

like chunks of lead and her hands could not cling to anything.

"I can't," she gasped. "I can't get in."

Sam was sobbing as he struggled with her. "Try, you've got to try. I'm pulling all I can. You can't die, you can't. And Andy needs someone to help him. Please *try*!"

She had a sudden thought of her father, and the look on his face if they were to call him and tell him Ellen had died in a senseless, stupid accident, just as her mother had died. *Not for me, God,* she thought in a sort of agony, *but for him.* And, somehow, she was given enough strength to grip Sam's hands, to get her knees against the boat, to gain the necessary leverage to get over the side and tumble in on top of Andy.

Sam turned immediately to the motor, which had begun to cough. He was openly crying as he fought it back into a regular rhythm.

"Do you know artificial respiration?" he yelled at Ellen. "Do you? He's not breathing."

She didn't waste her energy on words. She straddled the limp little body, wishing frantically that the boat was flatter on the bottom, that it weren't rolling. *Mouth-to-mouth resuscitation wasn't always best for drowning cases,* she thought through some fog that threatened to take over her mind. She had to get out the water that he had in his lungs. She turned his head and felt for his tongue to see that it was forward in his mouth. And then, with arms too heavy to work, she began to press and release, press and release. *Please, God,* she was saying inside her head, *please, God, don't let him die.*

"Put my parka over him—he's freezing," she gasped.

Sam obeyed without a word and put his own jacket around her, fastening it at the throat but leaving her arms free.

There was a gagging sound from Andy, and he vomited into the bottom of the boat.

"Pull his face out of it," Ellen wheezed. "He's starting to breathe. Maybe—"

But her words were stopped by another spasm of nausea from the little boy, and when he stopped vomiting, he was breathing with a ragged, uneven sound.

She sat in the bottom of the boat and tugged him up over her shoulder, like a baby, his head hanging down over her back. He was sick again on Sam's good jacket, but Ellen's thoughts were only jubilant ones.

"Bring it all up, Andy," she said. "You'll be okay."

"He must have swallowed it," Sam said. "Instead of breathing it in, he must have swallowed it."

Freezing, aching from the heavy weight of her little cousin, cramped from the position on the floor, Ellen looked up at Sam. There were marks of tears on his face, but already the fear was gone, and his cocky confidence was coming back. She looked away from him, sick with a sudden terrible anger. She had never in her life come close to wanting to smash at someone, to claw and bite. But she wanted to do all of these things to Sam. Just because Andy was breathing, just because God had given them a miracle and his brother hadn't drowned, Sam thought it was all over. He was home free! Well, he wasn't. She'd see to that. She'd tell Uncle Archie and she bet Sam would never get a chance to go out in the boat again. Not after what *she'd* tell.

She looked toward shore and was shocked to see that they had reached the dock, that there was the house and warmth and safety and punishment for Sam. If anything had happened to Andy—.

"You tell anyone what happened," Sam said, as though he could read her thoughts, "you breathe a single word of it—I know Andy won't—and I'll—I'll tell things about you that will ruin you—in our house and at school. I mean it. I'll make you sorry you ever set foot in this country."

She stared at him with her mouth open. He meant it. And sick and miserable and hurt as she was, she knew at last what was wrong with Sam. Mary Ann had been right. He was literally scared to death, but he knew only one way to cope with fear—and that was with threats and a pretense at bravado that was as phony as a three-dollar bill.

Ellen shifted Andy's weight, feeling the little body starting to struggle and stir.

"Okay," she choked out to Sam. "I won't tell, but not because I'm afraid of you. And certainly not because I care about you. Because I want you to wake up every morning of your life knowing that you almost killed your brother, and you're too stinking cowardly to admit it."

The boat bumped gently against the dock, and she saw Dave coming across the lawn at a run. They knew something was terribly wrong; Andy would never let anyone hold him, especially not like Ellen was doing.

7

Ellen was trying to struggle out of a dark and terrifying dream that was filled with wind and water and a pain that made it hard to breathe. She knew she was drowning and tried to cry out, but she could make no sound. She woke at last, relieved to discover that the pain was only the coughing that was strangling out of her chest. She had coughed for two days since the accident, until she was exhausted and every fresh spasm cut into her like knives.

She turned over, trying to get comfortable, but was suddenly aware that there was movement in the house, that lights were burning and voices were speaking rapidly and softly.

A fresh spasm of coughing shook Ellen, and her door was pushed open. Aunt Betty stood in the doorway, her hair disheveled, her face looking white and strained.

"Ellen, are you sick, honey? Do you feel all right?"

"It's just this cough," Ellen said, her voice raspy. "My chest hurts a little, but I don't feel sick. I was just going to get up and rub something on my chest and take another dose of that horrible medicine."

Aunt Betty didn't smile. She came quickly across the room and put her hand on Ellen's forehead. "No fever," she murmured in a thankful-sounding voice. "No fever, or only a touch at the most. Ellen, listen, honey, will you be okay if Uncle Archie and I leave for a little while?"

"Now? In the middle of the night?" Ellen said stupidly.

"It's Andrew," Aunt Betty said, and her voice seemed to catch and break a little, as though she were as young as Ellen. "He's really terribly sick. The doctor says we've got to get him into the hospital at Little Current. It's pneumonia, I guess. Plus the shock. Will you, honey? Will you be all right? The boys will be here, and I'll have Dave keep his door open so he can hear you if you call."

"I won't need anyone. I'm okay," Ellen said, ignoring the ache in her chest, the heaviness in her arms and legs. "Just go, Aunt Betty. Get him there as soon as possible. Don't let anything happen to him."

She had dragged Andrew out of the water, she had made him breathe again, she had held him over her shoulder as though he were her own baby, and she couldn't bear it that he was in danger again.

"Can I see him?" Ellen said, a new coughing spell making her choke on the words. "Can I see him for a minute?"

"Yes. Come on. Here, put on your slippers and warm robe. I can't have two children with pneumonia." Aunt Betty tried to make her voice light, but Ellen heard the pain in it.

Andrew was bundled up and lying on the couch, and evidently Uncle Archie had gone to get the car. Dave sat beside his little brother, holding him from falling from the couch, as Andy was tossing fretfully, throwing his arms, muttering with a hoarse little whisper. His cheeks were like fire, and his eyelashes were in sticky points on his cheeks where he had cried and the tears had matted them together.

Sam was sitting on another chair, but his face was white as paper, his lips trembling. Ellen could hardly bear to look at him. Ever since Andrew had been safely rescued, Sam had been unbearably cocky and smug. Maybe it was all a cover-up, as Mary Ann had said, but right now, Ellen didn't care and found it impossible to feel the least bit sorry for him. If he was suffering, then good! She hoped his heart hurt so bad that he could hardly bear it.

She knelt beside the couch. Andrew was the only little child she had ever known intimately, and she had delighted in his funny mixture of little boy and baby. She had felt amused by him and protective toward him, and she thought she couldn't bear to see him so sick. She really ought to be praying for him, but her feeling for Sam—a feeling bitter enough to be hate, she guessed—was using up what little energy she had.

"Will he be all right?" she begged Aunt Betty, trying to take one of the hot, wildly flailing little hands in her own. "Will he be okay?"

"Of course," Aunt Betty said firmly. "It's just a matter of getting him in where they can give him penicillin every few hours—or oxygen if he needs it. He'll be all right." But her eyes did not look directly at either Ellen or the two older boys. She was buttoning up her coat around her throat, and Ellen could see her hands trembling.

"Here's dad," Dave said. "I'll carry Andy out to the car. Sure you don't want me to go and help hold him?"

"No," Aunt Betty said. "You stay here with Ellen and the boys. I couldn't go with an easy heart if you weren't here."

Ellen wanted to say, *Go with them, Dave. They might need you.* But she felt too sick herself to be brave enough to say the words. If the cough got too bad, if the nightmare got unbearable, she wanted to know that Dave was in the house. Having only Sam there—for Phil was too young to really count—was worse than being alone.

She watched Dave carrying Andrew out the door, and her thoughts were a jumble of prayer and anger. *Please let him get well. Please let him get well.* But at the same time, *It ought to be Sam who is sick—not Andy.* Because, in spite of her grief, her bitterness was bigger than love.

During the few minutes before Dave came back in the house, there was absolute silence in the living room, except for the rough, hard sound of Ellen's cough. She turned, still on her knees, and looked steadily at Sam. For a minute he brazened it out, staring back at her, trying to steady his lips, but then his eyes dropped and he turned away. She saw his shoulders shake.

Cry, she thought, *go ahead and cry. You'll do more than that if Andy—* But her mind stopped before she even thought the word, and a kind of blackness filled her. Andy couldn't die. There had been enough death in her life. It couldn't happen again.

She struggled to her feet and, going the long way so she would not have to walk close to Sam, she went to the bathroom and got the cough medicine out of the medicine chest and took a large, bitter dose. Then she rubbed the pungent salve on her chest, feeling its warmth spread across her skin.

She did these things carefully and methodically, not because she really cared how she felt, but because she could not get sick and take anyone's attention away from Andrew. She absolutely did not dare be a burden on Aunt Betty or Uncle Archie.

She heard the outside door slam and heard Dave's voice telling Sam to go to bed. She wondered if Dave had seen Sam's tears and had wondered at them, but she was suddenly too tired to really care.

As she plodded toward her bedroom, Dave met her in the hall. "I'm going to bring you a heating pad," he said, "and a glass of hot lemonade. It's pretty foul-tasting, but mom insists it's good for you, and maybe it will help you sleep."

"I don't want to be a bother," she said in a dead little voice.

"Don't be dumb. How could you be a bother? Aren't you the one who—who saved Andy? And, anyway," he hurried on, "you wouldn't have been a bother anyhow. A guy expects these things with sisters and brothers."

Oh, David, Ellen thought foggily, *if you only know!*

Morning came at last. Ellen heard someone come in just as the sky was showing the first tints of dawn, and then she really slept as though she had been drugged. She never heard the three boys get up and leave for school; she never heard a sound until about ten o'clock, when the shrilling of the telephone cut through her sleep.

The closed door muffled Aunt Betty's voice, but Ellen could sense that there was a note of alarm in it. *Andrew must be worse.* She threw back the covers, feeling light headed and weak, but aware almost at once that her chest did not hurt so bad, and that the cough was looser and less painful.

She had only time to get her slippers and robe on when the door opened. Aunt Betty looked in at her, and she made no attempt to hide the tears that were streaking down her cheeks.

"Andy's worse," she said. "I came home to get some rest and left Uncle Archie there, and he just called. I've got to go in right away. But I can't leave you here alone."

"I'm okay," Ellen said, her voice coming out in a croak. "I sound awful, but honest, I'm better. My chest doesn't hurt, and my cough is better. I'll stay in bed all day and take the medicine and I won't get chilled or anything. I'm not a baby. You go to the hospital."

"Oh, Ellen," Aunt Betty said, and she opened her arms.

Ellen had never known the strange sensation of comforting an adult. When her mother died, her own grief had been so terrible that she had not been able to help her father. But now, it was natural and not at all embarrassing to go over to her aunt and put her arms around her as though she were a young girl.

"He'll be all right," Ellen said. "Don't cry, Aunt Betty. God will take care of him. I'm sure he will. God won't let anything happen."

Even as she said it, she wondered at her daring to say these words to an adult, and especially when both she and Aunt Betty knew that sometimes terrible things *did* happen.

But, amazingly, Aunt Betty seemed to be comforted by the words. "I know," she said in a clogged voice. "I *do* know. But bless you for reminding me."

"Then go on to the hospital—please do. I'll be okay. Honest!"

It took some persuading, but finally Aunt Betty left and Ellen was alone in the quiet old farmhouse.

Once more she did all the necessary things to make herself better, because it was essential for her to get well so she could help. She fixed some breakfast and took it into her room and crawled back into the warm bed, blessing Dave for providing the comfort of the heating pad. She had pulled the curtains open, so she ate her breakfast looking out at the water. Another light snow had fallen in the night and, in the shade of the spreading evergreens, it was still carpeting the ground with cold. The water looked gray and sullen, and Ellen thought she was beginning to understand why the islanders looked forward to the winter ice. Ice would never have this hard and threatening look.

Or maybe it was only the accident that made her feel this way. She hadn't made any effort to really think things through since the terrible minute when Andrew had slid right past her helpless gaze into the icy waves. But she knew she had to think it out. She had to come to some conclusion about Sam. She had to make up her mind whether or not she would tell the truth about what happened.

There had been no questioning at the time because the water *had* been rough, and everyone who lived here knew that accidents happened. Ellen had been dazed and weeping, and Aunt Betty had made her take a scalding hot bath and get into bed, while Uncle Archie was taking care of Andrew. There had simply been too much necessary action to be taken for anyone to think much or ask about *how* the accident had occurred.

And what would be achieved now by telling? Ellen asked herself, looking somberly out the window, feeling the silence and the loneliness crowding around her. *Isn't Sam being punished enough? And would I tell anyhow, just for the sake of getting Sam punished?*

She set the breakfast tray on the floor and leaned back against her pillows. Her eyes filled with tears, and she thought for just a few minutes that she was going to die of homesickness. It only lasted a short time, but it was a pain far worse than the pain in her chest had been last night. *Oh, daddy,* she thought, *if only you were here to tell me what to do.*

Daddy had said that God would always be near if she prayed, but it didn't seem to be working for her. Maybe she wasn't trying hard enough. She made herself become totally still, inside and out. And then she said out loud, "Please, dear God, show me what to do. I'm so scared. Show me what to do."

Her thoughts sorted themselves out of a jumble and began to come slowly and clearly. There was much more involved than just punishment for Sam. Aunt Betty and Uncle Archie had to be warned, because Sam might do it again. Maybe he wouldn't mean to; but when he felt the same stupid need to show off, to hide his fear with foolish risks, he just might do it again.

That was the whole trouble with Sam, Ellen thought. He couldn't be trusted to do what he ought to do—what he probably knew very well he should do. If his parents didn't know of his reckless actions, how could he be prevented from doing it again?

But if I tell, Ellen thought, *I'll only make things worse. It isn't only that he'll tell lies about me—and maybe he wouldn't, for he might have only been saying that to scare me—but what if I tell, and Andrew—and Andrew dies. How will Uncle Archie and Aunt Betty bear it, knowing that Sam killed his brother?*

The words were ugly in her mind. Did this mean that God didn't want her to tell? *But it isn't fair,* she thought. She tried to pray, but her feeling for Sam was so bitter that the prayers got tangled up with it and didn't come out as prayers at all. She finally slept, waking later to hear the telephone ringing. It was Aunt Betty.

"How is he?" Ellen said.

"Just the same," Aunt Betty said. "He's holding his own, and that's good."

"Can I do anything?" Ellen said. "I feel I ought to do something."

"Darling, you've done everything a girl could possibly do. Without you—" Aunt Betty's voice broke.

"Don't cry," Ellen begged. "He'll be all right. I'm sure he will.

"Just keep praying," Aunt Betty said.

"I will," Ellen promised. "I will."

She heard the school bus stopping late in the afternoon, and in a few minutes Dave and Phil came in, their faces strained and pale.

"We called mom at noon," Dave announced. "Have you talked to her since?"

"Just a little while ago," Ellen said. "He's holding his own, she said. That's good, she told me."

Phil made a strange little sound and then went toward his room. His door closed and Ellen pictured him throwing himself on the bed, quiet and solitary as Phil always was, but knowing as much pain as the rest of them.

Dave sat down on a chair. He tried to make his grin look natural, but Ellen could see the effort.

"You don't have to stay and talk to me," she said. "I'm all right. I can go to school tomorrow or the next day."

"But *I'm* not all right," Dave said. "I need a girl to talk to. Even a cousin will do."

"Thanks," she said, pretending to be indignant, knowing they were both putting on an act for the benefit of the other.

Suddenly Dave shot a swift glance at Ellen. "What really happened out in the boat, Ellen? Really, I mean."

She stared at him in silence. What had Dave sensed to ask this so abruptly? Had he seen the anger between her and Sam? And by the way, where *was* Sam?

"Where's Sam?" she asked.

"He stayed on the bus and went on into town. He's going to the hospital. But you didn't answer my question."

"I—I can't," she said. "Don't ask me, Dave."

"Who are you covering up for?" Dave asked, and his voice was hard, adult, uncompromising. "Sam? Andrew? Yourself? Who?"

She dropped her eyes and pleated the quilt between her fingers, and saw, to her surprise, that her hands were shaking.

"Did Andrew stand up?" Dave went on. "He knows the rules. Did he stand up?"

"No, no," she cried.

"Did you tease him or shove him?" he asked.

Her eyes flew up to blaze at his. "Dave! You know—"

"I know, I know," he said softly. "Then it's Sam. It wasn't just an accident?"

"I—I can't tell," she said.

"But why can't you tell?" Dave asked. "Did Sam threaten you? Are you afraid of him?"

"Afraid of him?" she said bitterly. "It's like being afraid of a gull because it makes a lot of noise."

"Then why?" Dave persisted.

So she told him. She told him everything—Sam's stupidity, Andrew's pitiful attempt at being brave so that he wasn't holding on, Sam's threat, her own great fear that if Aunt Betty and Uncle Archie knew of Sam's guilt and Andrew died, they would never be able to forgive him. But she also told of her conviction that Sam could not be really trusted not to repeat such actions. The words came out ragged and broken, but Dave listened patiently without comment. She saw a little knot of muscle work in his jaw, and she thought how odd that he would have the same reaction to tension her father did when they weren't blood relatives.

When the story was fully told, Dave sat in silence for a long time. When he spoke, his voice was soft, but she knew he was keeping it soft by great effort, that he wanted to shout and swear and maybe throw things.

"Don't think about it anymore," he said. "None of it is your fault, and Sam can't hurt you. If Andy gets worse—or even if—*when* he gets better, then I'll tell. They've got to know."

Dave got up from his chair. "You're a good little kid, Ellen," he said gently. "I'll take care of everything. You just rest and get better."

He turned and left the room. She lay awake for a long time and then she finally slept again.

Somehow, the evening passed. Mary Ann's father took the boys to the hospital, and Ellen slept most of the time from exhaustion. She was never quite sure when it was that the boys came home with the report that Andrew was just the same and that Sam was still at the hospital with his parents. Somehow, in spite of the grief and the worry, Ellen slept again.

The next time she woke up, she knew that something had changed. There was a feeling in the air, like electricity, something sharp enough to almost be touched. Her door creaked open and Aunt Betty was standing there.

"Are you awake?" she whispered.

"Yes," Ellen answered. "How is he?"

"He's better," Aunt Betty said. "He's much better. He's going to be all right."

Ellen felt the sag of her bed as her aunt sat down beside her and gathered her into a fierce hug. They cried together, and then finally they could smile and talk, and Aunt Betty could tell her how it was and that the fever was broken and Andy was sleeping peacefully. Uncle Archie had stayed and was sleeping on a couch in the hospital's family room, but was only a gesture, really. Andy was going to make it.

"Ellen," Aunt Betty said at last, speaking slowly, softly, almost hesitantly, "Sam told us what happened. He said he threatened you. Is that why you didn't tell?"

"No, I thought you wouldn't be able to bear it if Andy—if he didn't get well and you knew Sam was to blame."

A noise at the door jerked both of them around. Sam was standing there and Dave was behind him. Sam's face was younger looking than Phil's. His eyes were swollen, and his mouth looked as though he had bitten his lip until it bled.

Ellen saw Dave's hand shove Sam's shoulder.

"I'm sorry, Ellen," Sam said, his voice coming out like a little boy's hiccup. "I'm sorry."

"It's all right, Sam," she said in an expressionless voice. "All that matters is that Andy's going to get well."

Dave's voice was very soft. "If *I* were you," he said to Sam, "I think I'd want to kiss her."

"You can make me apologize," Sam said, "but

there's a limit."

He ducked under Dave's arm and disappeared. But Ellen hardly noticed. Her eyes met Dave's and Aunt Betty's with a great gladness. Andy was going to be all right!

It was only later, just before she went to sleep, that she realized nothing had changed for her. In spite of everything, Sam still had not been turned into a friend.

8

Firelight made flickering little shadows on the wall, and Ellen pushed away her algebra book to concentrate on the shimmering spots of light and dark. She was in Mary Ann's living room, a room where she now felt as much at home as at the Ludlows, and the girls had been working together on an assignment that seemed endless and dull.

Mary Ann looked up from her book and followed Ellen's example. They had been lying on their stomachs in front of the fire, which was pleasant but uncomfortable, and now they both rolled over and lay full length, staring at the ceiling.

"Do you think it's possible to be in love when

you're fourteen?" Mary Ann asked.

"My dad says Juliet was only fourteen when she fell in love with Romeo," Ellen said. "I was in love last year with a boy in our apartment building. But he never even kissed me," she finished gloomily.

"I just wondered," Mary Ann said in a dreamy voice.

"Are you in love?" Ellen asked abruptly. "With Sam?"

"Oh, I don't know." But Mary Ann refused to meet Ellen's eyes. "He's—no one understands Sam. He's sweet."

Ellen laughed. "I have a hard time thinking of him as 'sweet,' but I'll admit he's good-looking. Almost as good-looking as Dave."

Mary Ann rolled back on her stomach and propped her chin on her hands. "Is Dave taking Patty Marsh to the Christmas skating party?"

Ellen nodded. "I think so. He didn't say for sure, but I heard him talking on the phone, and she's awfully friendly to me all of a sudden."

Mary Ann giggled. "It's a nice way to get to spend time with the Ludlow boys—be nice to their cousin."

"Oh, shut up," Ellen said absently. "You know I don't mean you."

"Maybe Sam will come over to get you tonight," Mary Ann said.

"Aunt Betty will have to make him," Ellen said. "It's usually Dave who comes after me."

"Down to Rachael's, yes," Mary Ann conceded. "But Sam likes to come here. Haven't you ever noticed?"

"I guess," Ellen said.

She was quiet for a few minutes, and then she spoke in a voice that was a little irritated. "I don't know why one of the boys has to come after me, anyhow. It's only down the road. And there aren't any drunks or roughnecks around here like down home. What do they think will get me—the Abominable Snowman?"

"You aren't used to this kind of weather," Mary Ann said. "People can fall or get off the road into a field and really get lost. It's so dark and the snow is funny. I wouldn't like to walk alone at night."

"Is that why Sam walks you home from my place?" Ellen said, darting a mischievous look at Mary Ann.

Mary Ann grinned, refusing to be embarrassed.

Ellen was touched with sudden curiosity. She wondered if Sam had ever kissed Mary Ann. If so, how would he be—silly and smart acting, or gentle like he had been that day, cradling the small bird in his hands. She was dying to ask, but she didn't have the nerve.

"Listen, Mary Ann, about Patty. Patty and Dave. Do you think they like each other?"

"She's really crazy about him," Mary Ann said. "But I don't think he feels the same way. Dave's funny."

"He is not!" Ellen's defense of Dave was quick and hot. "He's absolutely great! If he doesn't like Patty, there's got to be a reason."

"She's the prettiest, most popular girl in the thirteenth grade," Mary Ann pointed out.

"That doesn't mean anything," Ellen said. "Maybe he doesn't really like girls."

"All Ludlow boys like girls," Mary Ann said with a note of authority. "Even Phillip has a crush on that little Bonner girl in his room, and he's only twelve. Wait'll Andy gets old enough. He's going to be the best looking of them all."

"Good old Andy," Ellen said, her voice soft, remembering the fear of nearly losing him. "I think I'll use my magic power and turn him into a handsome prince and marry him myself."

Mary Ann poked her in derision, and they laughed together.

"Well, anyhow," Mary Ann said, "if Dave is taking Patty to the dance, he must like her a little. I never see him with anyone else. I mean, anyone special. Sometimes he talks to Debbie Wawaskesh in the halls, but that doesn't mean anything."

"What do you mean, it 'doesn't mean anything'?" Ellen asked, partly out of curiosity but partly out of a sudden apprehension. She would not, she simply would not believe that there was any real prejudice against Indians up here. If there were, if the same kind of intolerance existed here that was so common in Washington, then why had she come?

Why did anyone come to Canada to find a new and more honest life if prejudice could be found here, too? She simply wouldn't think about it. It couldn't be true, anyhow. Hadn't the Ludlows all been marvelous to Rachael? Weren't Sam and Dave really friendly to Tom and Fred Enoss? Not just polite but really friendly. She looked at Mary Ann, feeling breathless, begging her silently not to say anything that would shatter her dream.

Mary Ann looked at her in the glow of the firelight, and for a few minutes she was silent. Then she smiled, and her face had that curiously adult look Ellen had seen on it before.

"I didn't mean anything," Mary Ann said. "That was dumb of me. I expect Dave and Debbie are really good friends. They're the top two kids in their class, so it'd only be natural."

"She wants to go to a university," Ellen confided, feeling relief wash through her. Her fears had been unfounded, as she should have known they would be. "But she lives with her grandfather, and he's old. I hope she gets some kind of a scholarship."

"If her grades are good enough," Mary Ann said, "the Indian Affairs people will help her. They do that."

Ellen wanted to say, *But why must her scholarship come through the Indian Affairs people? Why can't she just get it because she's a good student?* But that was the way Clarisse would think, and there wasn't any similarity between the situation here and Clarisse's situation, so she put the thought out of her mind.

Just then, Sam came, and their talk was finished. He said they had time for a snow battle if the girls weren't too chicken to come out in the cold. They ran for their wraps, and the evening ended for Ellen with laughter and snow down her neck and the unexpected sight of seeing Sam wash Mary Ann's face with snow and then, thinking his cousin wasn't looking, dropping a quick kiss on Mary Ann's smiling mouth. So—that's how it was!

Oddly, enough, after Ellen was home and in bed, it wasn't Mary Ann and Sam she kept seeing behind her closed eyes, but Dave and Patty Marsh and Debbie Wawaskesh. She was trying to remember how Dave had looked when she had seen him with either girl, but her mind was a blank.

Her last thought before she slept was of Stephen Upton, the boy in her Washington apartment building whom she had mentioned so casually to Mary Ann. She hadn't even thought of him much since she came to the island, but she was suddenly stabbed with a small prick of loneliness—not for Steve, exactly—but for the way she used to feel about him. She wondered if he were changing any as he grew up. She hoped that if he were, it would be in a way that would make him a little like Dave.

The night of the high school skating party was

bitterly cold and the ground was white with a cover of snow that Uncle Archie said was really unusual for early December. The black sky—Ellen could never get enough of looking at this black sky that was never smeary or pale like the sky is over large cities—was frosted with a million stars. Dave insisted that Ellen come to the party and had practically made Sam agree to skate with her, too, so that she would have a good time. Ellen felt awkward about going, but Dave said she was being silly to worry about whether or not she had a date. Lots of kids went without partners, he said.

"You can sit in the front seat with Patty and me," he had said the evening he had coaxed her to go. "That way, Sam can make out with Mary Ann in the back seat."

"Aw, shut up," Sam said, but his face got a tinge of pink in it.

"David!" Aunt Betty said. "Don't, for heavens sakes put ideas in Sam's head. He and Mary Ann are too young for such goings-on, and I won't even let Ellen go if you can't all settle down."

Ellen hardly heard for wondering why in the world Dave would want her to sit with him and Patty. Nobody could say *he* was too young for "such goings-on."

On the way to the party, in the front seat beside Patty, who smelled simply delicious, Ellen tried not to feel like a fifth wheel. She hoped that Dave wouldn't be stuck with her all evening, and she half wished that she had stayed at home.

Sam and Mary Ann were talking a blue streak in the back seat, arguing the merits of curling teams. Ellen was still astonished at the passion all these people had for curling, that odd game played on the ice with a large stone. But the three in the front were quiet. Ellen kept snatching quick looks at Patty, wondering how Dave could help being in love with her. She was pretty, and everytime she looked at Dave there was something in her eyes that would melt an iceberg. *Oh, well, it's not my concern,* Ellen thought. *Maybe Dave is absolutely mad about her, and he just doesn't show his emotions.*

To her delight, the evening went better than her wildest hopes. True, Dave skated with her several times, but she really had the feeling that he wanted to, that he wasn't embarrassed because she was his cousin and only in ninth grade, but that he enjoyed being with her.

Sam skated with her once, too, in one of the fast numbers, and she found herself laughing with delight at the swift, light way he moved, the strong sureness of his hands. He was grinning and relaxed, and for those few minutes she felt almost as comfortable with him as she did with Dave. In the midst of one dizzy whirl, she had the sudden thought that if Sam were always like this, there would be nothing in her way if she wanted to stay on the island forever.

A number of other boys asked her to skate. She

thought that Dave probably did a little persuading, or maybe the fact that she was still a little different from the island girls helped. At any rate, the boys were friendly and the evening passed in a whirl of joy.

When it came time to leave, Ellen assumed that Dave would take them out to the farms, and then go back into town with Patty, but to her astonishment, they drove directly to the Marsh home from the dance. Ellen offered to get out, but Patty spoke quickly.

"No," she said. "I'll slide out under the steering wheel. If Dave is going to walk to the door with me, that is."

Her voice sounded odd, and Ellen couldn't figure out if she were angry or on the verge of tears. Her voice wobbled in a way that could be either one.

"Don't be silly," Dave said, but he didn't sound as calm as usual. "Of course, I'm walking in with you. Come on, slide under the wheel. Ellen, keep an eye on those two in the back seat. "I'll be right back."

Ellen watched him walk beside Patty up to her porch, and she noticed that he didn't even take her hand.

She felt shy turning around, but she simply had to ask a question before Dave came back.

"I'm not being snoopy," she started apologetically, turning toward the two in the backseat. "But what's with Dave? How come he asked her to the skating party and then acts so—so casual? I mean it doesn't make sense."

Sam cleared his throat and then spoke hesitantly, as though he might be breaking a confidence and was doing so with reluctance.

"I don't think he exactly asked her. I think she asked him."

"You're putting me on," Ellen said, staring in amazement.

Even Mary Ann looked startled. "I can't imagine Patty Marsh having to ask *anyone* to a party," she said. "She's so fabulous-looking. I mean, granted Dave is special, still . . ."

Sam just grunted and a silence filled the car. In a very few minutes, Dave was back. As they started out, Ellen was suddenly reminded of the way Dave had looked and acted that first night he had picked her up at Enoss's house. As a matter of fact, *every* time he picked her up at the reservation. There was always an excitement that certainly wasn't there now. He didn't look like a boy ought to look who had just kissed a pretty girl good night.

But when they left the reservation, he did.

Ellen sat in stunned silence. What was it Mary Ann had said that night by the fire? "Sometimes he talks to Debbie Wawaskesh in the halls, but that doesn't mean anything."

Or did it?

The drive back to the farm was a quiet one. Dave poked her once and said, "You aren't keeping Mary

Ann busy talking like you're supposed to."

Mary Ann spoke up clearly. "Don't worry. We're only thinking."

"About what?" Dave asked carelessly.

But no one answered him, and he didn't act like he expected them to.

9

Ellen's father arrived the Friday evening before Christmas, and the first few hours were so filled with joy and confusion that Ellen had no time to sort out her thoughts or feelings, other than to know that she was happy enough to burst.

Next morning, they all gathered around the breakfast table, and it was hard to tell what shone brighter—the cold blue sky reflected on the crystal lake or the faces in the sun-filled room.

Now, Ellen thought, *we are all together. I wish, oh, I wish it could always be like this. If only daddy didn't have to go home.* It wasn't until now, this minute, that she really realized how terribly much she had missed him. It was partly the way he talked, she discovered all at once in the middle of one of his stories. No one else talked quite the same, with so much humor and with such a bookish manner. The Ludlows were talkative, but they didn't possess her father's wit or wisdom. Ellen felt a faint tinge of disloyalty at the mental comparison. It was just that she hadn't realized how much she *needed* the kind of talking her father did. Maybe that's why some of the kids still called her a Yankee, not so much because of a difference in accent, but because she was bound to talk a lot like her father. It was a strange thought, and she felt curiously upset by it, as though she shouldn't be thinking such things. Being fourteen and belonging to two families was terribly hard, she decided suddenly.

"Ellen and I are going to go for a walk," Mr. Ramsey announced, darting a quick look at Ellen, obviously aware of her silence. "She's going to show me this winter wonderland she keeps raving about."

"I'll come, too," Andy offered. "I know where the easiest paths are."

"No, you stay right here," Aunt Betty said. "Ellen knows where to go, and she and her father want to talk. Besides, I need a boy to run over to Trevors for me."

Ellen shot a grateful look at her aunt. Aunt Betty could always be counted on to handle things just right.

But when, booted and scarved, she and her father were out alone in the snow, walking down the snowmobile paths to the lake shore, she felt strangely shy, as though she didn't really know where to begin.

Her father spoke in a casual way. "I've never seen you look better, Ellen. Country life must really agree with you. You don't have to tell me you're happy; it shines all over your face."

"A lot of that is because you're here," Ellen said truthfully. "Nobody's happy all the time."

He slid a look at her. "I thought maybe you would be. Up here where life is simple and good and Aunt Betty is always around."

"Aunt Betty isn't mom," Ellen said soberly, almost as though she were really admitting it for the first time. "I think for a little while I almost felt as though she was. They look so much alike, and Aunt Betty is so great. And well, I guess I tried to pretend everything was like it used to be. You know?"

"I know," her father said softly. "But nothing will ever be the same as it used to be. You have to take Aunt Betty for what she is, which is really quite, quite different from your mother. When I met them in college, most people couldn't even tell them apart. For me, there was never any problem."

"That's because you—because you were in love

with one of them," Ellen said hesitantly. She had never talked to her father before about such personal things.

He smiled his calm, warm smile at her. "Yes, I was. I still am. That's something you might never be able to understand. I've never quit loving your mother, and I never will. Never." His voice faltered a little, and Ellen looked away quickly.

"But," he went on, "although the saying is trite, it's true that life *does* go on. And it's my own personal discovery that a man—at least *this* man—is capable of loving more than once. Do you understand what I'm trying to tell you, honey?"

"That you're in love with Frances." Her voice was expressionless and she fought to keep it that way.

"Yes, I am. Not just in a companionship way—just friends—but really in love. I suppose it seems totally impossible to you that a man forty years old—"

She tried to laugh and her voice caught in her throat. "No harder for me to think that, I guess, than for you to believe that someone my age could be in love."

"Nicely put," he said with surprised satisfaction. "Are you in love, Ellen?"

"I was once," she said, as though it had been a very long time ago. "But Sam is, I think, and Mary Ann. Really, I guess. If you can believe *that*, I should be able to believe about you. Does Frances love you?"

"She says she does."

There was a long silence, and Ellen put her mittened hand above her eyes to shield them from the glare of the ice that was thickening on the lake. She was trying to see Frances in her mind, to hear her, to remember how she felt about her. Frances wasn't terribly pretty, Ellen thought with some confusion, but she had a marvelous sense of humor, and when she laughed, everyone in the room felt happy. Frances was really all right. It was just . . .

"I want to marry her." Mr. Ramsey's words were quiet. "But I want *you* to say it's all right. I want you to approve as much as possible. She won't be—can't be—a substitute for your mother. But she can be herself, and I think she could do a great deal to make your life good."

After a few seconds Ellen said miserably, "I think it's okay if you marry Frances. Only—"

"Only what?"

"Only if I decide to stay here, you might think it's because of her."

"And it wouldn't be?" His voice was very grave.

"No, no, honestly. It's just that things are so—well, I can't tell you how I feel about the Ludlows—but especially about the island."

They had reached the edge of the lake, and they found a sheltered place behind the boathouse where the sun, shining against the white boards, made it almost warm. There was a wooden sawhorse there, and they sat down on it, close together, their shoulders touching.

"You haven't found any of the intolerance you objected to so violently at home?" he asked.

"No," she said quickly, sharply. "No, not a single bit!"

He glanced at her with a slight smile. "'Me thinks the lady doth protest too much,'" he quoted wryly.

"Oh, I suppose there are a few things that aren't just perfect. But *nothing* like it is at home. Next to Mary Ann, my best friend is Rachael Enoss. Nobody objects."

"I never objected to your being friends with Clarisse," he said mildly. "Clarisse was the one who got—what? Uppity? Is Rachael likely to get uppity?"

"Of course not," Ellen said emphatically.

She had thought she would be able to tell her father about Debbie Wawaskesh and what she was beginning to suspect about Dave's feeling for the lovely Indian girl. But she found she couldn't put it into words. In the first place, she didn't even know if it was true. It was all based on guesswork. In the second place, she didn't want to hear any adult make condescending remarks about it. Not even her father. Whatever the situation was, it was Dave's business, no one else's.

Mr. Ramsey put his arm around Ellen's shoulders and drew her up and held her close. "I know we're not perfect, we Americans. I know we have lots of ugly faults and stupid ideas. But I happen to believe in being an American. I was hoping you would, too."

"I'm sorry, daddy. It just seems more honest up here. Fairer. Maybe I'll change my mind, but I don't think so."

Mr. Ramsey didn't answer right away, and some of the happiness Ellen had felt at the breakfast table deserted her. She was hurting her father, and she knew it. But when she thought of going back to the prejudice, and the tragedies that made headlines every night, and the look of suspicion and scorn in Clarisse's face, she just thought she couldn't stand it.

"And what about church?" Mr. Ramsey said, shaping the words carefully. "Are you still angry at—what did you call it?—the phoniness of the church?"

"I haven't thought about it much," she admitted in a low voice. "I don't really go to church all that often up here."

"But you wrote once of being able to talk about—I think you said 'religious things'—with your friend Rachael. Don't you go to church with her?"

"Oh, no, daddy. She goes to church on the reservation. When I go, I go here in Little Current."

"Where the white people go," he finished for her. "Is that why you stay home?"

She felt her face flushing. There had been nothing noble at all in her staying away from church. It had been sheer laziness. And she hadn't even thought about the fact that Aunt Betty's church was primarily white, not until Daddy had said the bald, ugly words. *It wasn't fair of him*, she thought rebelliously.

"And have you stopped talking to God, too?" Mr. Ramsey asked gently.

Her face was still hot, but she made her voice stiff with a kind of dignity. "I don't break my promises."

Her father smiled. "Sweetheart, I don't want you to pray just to keep a promise to me. I want God to be there when you need him. Familiar, not a stranger."

Ellen relaxed. "Believe me," she said, "when I was fishing Andy out of that icy water, I wasn't praying because of any promises I had made."

Mr. Ramsey grinned. "Good! That's the way I want it to be."

"And—and if I do decide to stay up here, you'll forgive me?" Ellen asked after a few minutes of silence.

Her father stood up and smiled down at her. "We won't even worry about it now. Winter is really only beginning, and you're still on a sort of holiday basis. If by spring you feel just like you do now, I won't be the heavy father. I'll let you stay, at least for a while. But you'll have to come home for long visits. You'll come when Frances and I get married, won't you?"

"I wouldn't miss it for the world," she said fervently. "I promise!"

They really never seemed to find any time for another confidential talk during the week her father was on the island. They just had too many things to do. They rode down to the reservation and visited with the Enoss family, and Ellen was delighted at how comfortable her father seemed to be with Rachael and her brothers and parents.

She managed to get permission to take him through the school on an inspection tour, and she showed off everything with a pride that was almost like ownership.

The whole family took him out on the snowmobile and even introduced him to curling. He was clumsy in his curling boots and seemed totally unable to throw the heavy stone along the slick ice, even though Phil swept furiously, trying to make a path completely free of obstacles. Ellen laughed until she cried, watching her father, but she felt no inclination this time to compare his clumsiness with the agile skill of Uncle Archie, Aunt Betty, and the boys. After all, she was not very good on the ice herself, and she knew that in this respect, the Ludlows were a hundred times superior to their American relatives. But her father and she could do other things, she thought comfortably. Everyone couldn't be perfect in everything.

Best of all, of course, was Christmas Eve. They went into town to a church service, and Ellen was surprised to discover that there was only happiness in her when she walked down the aisle and looked at the fragrant pine branches piled at the altar of the little church. The carols rang through the air with a silver sound, and Ellen sang the old, familiar words with a pleasure she hadn't expected.

Impulsively, she thrust her hand into her father's hand. "I wish Frances were here," she whispered. "Then it would really be perfect."

She meant it, too. She knew, in that minute, that Frances's presence would make her father happy, and his happiness would, in turn, rub off on Ellen. It was something she had never quite known before, and the discovery of it was lovely.

Mr. Ramsey squeezed her hand, and the smile he gave her was the kind of smile one adult might give another. In a way, it was the nicest Christmas present she gave and received.

They exchanged gifts when they got home, and Ellen was nearly overwhelmed by all she received. Most precious was a thin silver bracelet from daddy, and of course books, which he gave her every year, and from David a small wooden carving of a deer. She held it in her hands, loving the smooth, polished sheen of it, marveling at the dainty, thin legs, the branched, fragile antlers.

"Where in the world did you get it?" she asked.

"One of the Indian men carved it," he said carelessly. "I was able to talk him into selling it. Do you like it?"

"I love it," she said.

It wasn't at all like the Indian things that were made for the summer tourist trade. It was truly an exquisite little piece of art, and she wondered whose hands had labored so long and carefully over the little creature. She looked up into Dave's face, and her heart jumped a little. She thought she knew.

Frances had sent a sweater that was a lovely raspberry shade, and after all the packages were opened, Ellen just sat looking rapturously at everything.

"I feel rich," she confided, looking at everyone with a wide smile. "Rich as Midas."

And as happy as a king, she thought. *Or queen. Or, maybe I don't really know what happiness is. Maybe I'm just greedy and like to get presents and want everyone to like me. I wish it could be Christmas Eve forever,* she wished. *Forever and forever.*

Her father had to leave two days after Christmas, and Ellen really thought at the last minute that she simply could not let him go. She hadn't told him about anything that really mattered—not about Patty Marsh or Debbie Wawaskesh or how Andy's accident had really happened and how unfriendly Sam still was at times. Except for those few minutes by the boathouse, all the conversation had been casual and light.

And who can I talk to when he's gone? she thought with sudden panic as his plane was announced in Sudbury. *Not anyone, unless it's Dave. But do I even dare talk to Dave about any of it? Wouldn't he think I was sticking my nose in where I had no business? Maybe his feelings for Patty and Debbie are just the same. Maybe—* But she knew there was a difference, and she suddenly realized that what upset her so terribly about it all was that Dave was being so secretive about Debbie. Why? *Why?*

At least, she thought in a minute of fear, *things were open at home. People admitted they hated each other.*

The thought hit her like a blow, and she staggered a little under the impact of it. *Oh, no,* she whispered inside her secret heart. *Please let everything be the way it ought to be.*

Her father's hug was so hard that she gasped a little, and she felt the wetness of her tears against his face.

"Be good, darling," he whispered. "Come home for Easter. We'll plan the wedding for then if you think it's okay."

She nodded, afraid to trust her voice. Then he kissed her hard and sprinted for his plane. She stood, feeling the tears sting on her face because of the cold, and she wondered what she was doing—standing there in the middle of an airport, watching her own father leave to go hundreds of miles away.

She felt someone take her hand, and she looked up to see Dave smiling at her. "Come on back in the building before you freeze. We wanted to give you a minute alone with him, but we're almost afraid you'll change your mind at the the last minute and fly away."

She shook her head mutely. Then, holding his hand as though she were a child, she started across the snow-covered concrete.

"Dave," she said, not planning to say the words at all, "did Pete Wawaskesh carve my little deer?"

Dave stopped and looked at her. "You see too much," he said, but his eyes were warm. "Yes, it was Pete. How did you know?"

"I didn't," she said. "I guessed."

"I'll tell you all about it," he said. "About how he happened to carve it and how he feels about it, sometime when we're alone. Okay?"

"Okay," she said and trotted along beside him, slowly losing the emptiness that had washed through her when her father disappeared from view. There was still Dave for her comfort.

10

When the snow had begun to fall in November and December, Ellen had been completely enchanted with the wonder of the northern winter. She had known only the slush and discomfort of Washington snow, and she was hardly able to remember the deeper snows of Pennsylvania, so she was terribly excited at first over the purity, the depth, the excitement of snow that fell and did not melt away—snow that could be tunneled through or packed down or floundered into. But by mid-February the excitement had begun to pall.

She tried to attribute it to midwinter blues, to the fact that school always dragged between New

Year Day and Easter, but she finally had to accept that a lot of it was due to the fact that there was just simply *nothing* to do that did not deal with snow. One either went snowmobiling or curling or skating or tobogganing—or one stayed home.

She was sitting on the window seat in her room one afternoon, chin propped on her hand, thinking about all of this when Dave came by her door. He glanced in and whistled at her. She looked up and grinned, knowing that her gloomy face must have given her mood away.

"Problems?" he said.

She shook her head emphatically. "No, just feeling a little glum. February is a yucchy month."

"Valentine's Day comes in February," Dave said. "And so do all of your presidents' birthdays. And—and—"

"See!" she said. "Even you can't think of anything exciting."

"Curling," he said, and grinned sympathetically.

"I'm an absolute waste at curling," Ellen said despondently. "I have weak ankles and a lousy sense of timing, and that crazy stone always acts like it's nailed to the ice for *me*, but it skims along like a feather for all of you."

"You have to be born to curling," Dave said solemnly, but there was laughter in his eyes. "You were probably born to something lots more artistic and not nearly so strenuous."

"Does it show so much?" Ellen asked, hoping he

would erase all of her gloom with wise and witty words.

"It shows," he said briefly. There were times when Ellen wished Dave were not quite so honest. Most of the time, his honesty and dependability were treasures beyond price, but once in a while, she thought, the truth really hurt.

"I'm sorry," she said. "I try."

He came across the room and sat on the window seat beside her. On the middle windowsill, the little wooden deer he had given her for Christmas glowed softly in the winter light. Ellen and Dave both seemed to see it at the same time.

"Still like him?" Dave said casually.

"Love him!" Ellen said fervently. "I keep him here so I can see him first thing every morning. And even at night, when I wake up, he makes a tiny shadow against the snow outside. He's my favorite thing, I think. I call him Keneche."

"Where in the world did you get that name?" He sounded surprised.

"I made it up. It sounds kind of Indianish, doesn't it?"

"Very," he said. "As if you really knew the language."

She glanced at him shyly out of the corner of her eyes. "You said one time you'd tell me how he—Pete Wawaskesh—felt about the deer, but you never did."

"Well, I could try, I guess," Dave said. "But it's

tough to really understand old Pete, and tougher to describe him."

"Do you know him very well?"

"Pretty well," Dave's tone was casual, but there was something on his face that wasn't casual at all. "He used to take me fishing when I was a little kid. He was a guide for tourists and he used to let me go along to help rig rods and pull up anchor and so on. He taught me everything I know about fishing and water and boats."

Ellen looked at him wide-eyed. "I thought Uncle Archie taught you," she said.

"Dad's a farmer, not a sportsman. He doesn't have time. Oh, he hunts a bit in the fall. But, no, Pete was my teacher. Still is, in some ways. Only, he's getting old and he's starting to forget. It's awful for a man like that to get old."

She sat in silence for a minute, and then she said, "But about the deer. Tell me about that."

Dave hesitated. "Well, he loves deer," he began. "I mean, really loves them. He kills some for eating, but he would never hurt one or torment one or kill for sport. So when he carved this little deer, he tried to make it so beautiful that whoever got it would feel the love. Like a blessing. That's all."

Ellen picked up the deer with reverent fingers. She smoothed the satiny wood, which she had done so often that it had taken on a deeper sheen from her fingers. A sudden thought struck her.

"You didn't buy it from him, did you? He gave it to you. He wanted *you* to feel the love and the blessing."

An odd wash of red ran up over Dave's cheeks and forehead. "You see too much, like I've told you before. But not everything. I told him about you, and he agreed I should give it to you. He's making me another one."

She touched the little deer to her cheek. "I'll feel really blessed wherever I am," she said. "Forever and ever."

"Don't be a dope," he said. "If you get all hung up over it, I'll take it away from you. I just want you to have it because it's so beautiful, and because I wanted you to know that the cheap stuff the Indians make for the summer tourists isn't their real art. Some of them are really good. Old Pete is. He handles a knife like it was an alive thing."

"I'd like to meet him someday," Ellen said. "Do you suppose I ever will?"

"Sure," Dave said carelessly. "I'll take you over someday. In the spring." He laughed a little. "If old Pete lives till spring, that is. Every winter he's positive he'll never make it through until the ice melts."

Ellen joined the laughter. "I know exactly how he feels. Sometimes I'm not sure I'll make it through myself until the ice melts. Does it really melt, Dave, or was last summer just a dream?"

Dave pulled her hair and got up lazily from the

window seat. "You'll make it," he said. "Tomorrow is Valentine's Day, and after that, spring starts seeming like a possibility. In the meantime, tonight is one of the biggest curling games of the winter. Both mom and dad are playing. You're coming, aren't you?"

"Naturally," Ellen said. "Even if I get frostbite on both ears."

"Wear two hats," Dave advised and turned to leave. "I might even see you there. Who are you sitting with?"

"Mary Ann," she said. "Unless Sam deduces her away like he does other times."

"*Se*duces, goose," Dave said, laughing at her like any older brother. "Well, Sam's the one who could do it. You'll find someone else. You know lots of kids now."

"Wish Rachael would come," Ellen said, "but Tom can't get the car tonight."

"Don't worry," Dave said. "You'll find someone interesting."

The curling matches were exciting and fun, and Aunt Betty's team was really playing a superb game—Ellen had learned enough about curling to follow the movements of the stone and to know when a goal was imminent. But right in the middle of a play, she discovered that she was cold, and what was far worse, bored. The first dozen times she had attended curling matches, she had found them honestly exhilarating and fun. But slowly, so slowly that she had been really unaware of it, her enthusiasm had dwindled until she realized, all at once, that she really didn't want to watch curling two or three nights a week. Once a week, maybe, but no more. And she certainly couldn't stay at home on the farm all alone. *How grim,* she thought, more in disgust at herself than at the game. *Who would ever think the city girl in me would come out like this?*

She decided to take a little walk through the crowd, trying to find some of the girls from school, or even Phil and Andy. Mary Ann, with an honestly apologetic look, had disappeared long ago with Sam. It occurred to Ellen, not for the first time, that if Sam had any guts, he'd ask Mary Ann to come with him and not let Ellen make plans to be with Mary Ann and then be left alone. Oh, well, Sam was Sam, and nothing was going to change him.

She moved through the dense line of people who lined the rink and walked out of the arena where fewer people were. Some of the folks were just standing and talking, occasionally stamping their feet to keep them warm. Ellen's ears felt tingly and she wished that she had thrown vanity to the wind and taken Dave's advice about two caps. She looked around, able to recognize faces in the dim light, but there was no one she knew well enough to ask them to sit with her.

A shock of homesickness ran through her body like a physical blow, and she stood almost gasping for breath. Then it passed, and she looked a little dazedly around her, seeing the things that had grown familiar and comfortable over the months. She took a deep breath, feeling absurdly like one feels after a short, painful bout of toothache—remembering the pain but relieved that it is gone.

She had been so absorbed in what she was thinking and feeling that she had moved farther from the crowd than she realized. Her feet were silent in the snow, and she walked past a large tree and got two paces beyond it before she realized that there was someone standing in its shadow. It was not one person but two, only they had been standing in such a close embrace that they had been, for the first second, like one person. At the sound of Ellen's involuntary little gasp, the two shadows had jerked apart and had become two people—a tall, slender boy and a small, graceful girl. They stood in such startled stillness that Ellen felt there was more than embarrassment here. There was discomfort, if not actual fear.

In a way, she had known who they were even while they were still one blended, dark shadow close in each other's arms. Her heart had known. But her mind took several seconds to grasp the truth. It was like slow motion in a movie, and she knew her mouth hung open as her mind accepted and verified the fact that the two people facing her, like young animals at bay, were Dave and Debbie.

"I—I'm sorry," Ellen stammered, and her heart pounded as though she had been running. "I didn't mean to—mean to butt in like this. I was just walking and not thinking."

For a second they were silent, and Ellen thought in confusion, *Why am I so surprised? Didn't I guess it all along? Didn't I somehow know?* But still her heart jerked in shock.

"You were the one person I didn't expect to pry," Dave said.

"Dave, I *wasn't* prying," Ellen pleaded. "Honest."

"Of course you weren't," Debbie said. "We should not have—have trusted a tree so close to so many people."

"There are always people," Dave said, "and trees that are never wide enough."

Ellen had never heard that tone in Dave's voice, and she felt as though she were simply shriveling up inside. "I'm sorry," she said again. "I'm so sorry."

Debbie moved quickly and put her arm through Ellen's. "I'm glad you came," she said simply. "I've wanted Dave to tell you for a long time."

"Tell me what?" Ellen said.

"That— " Debbie's eyes turned to Dave.

"That I love her," Dave said quietly. "That she loves me."

The words were not silly kid words, they bore no relationship to the kind of puppy-love actions of Sam and Mary Ann. They were so starkly simple that they seemed to be the very essence of truth.

Then why all the mystery? Ellen thought. *Why the dark tree and the hiding of what was such a natural thing?* To her, it just seemed completely right to see Debbie and Dave together.

"But why is it so secret?" Ellen said. "I mean, why have you been hiding it all this time?"

"Because—" Debbie began, but Dave put a gentle hand over her mouth.

"Look, Ellen, it's something we just can't talk about now. There are reasons—believe me, there are good reasons—and we have to keep it a secret awhile longer. Will you help us? Keep it a secret, I mean?"

She stared from one to the other. Debbie looked almost frightened, and there was something about Dave that was different. As if he weren't sure of himself, not sure of anything. As though he were desperately, deadly serious in asking for her cooperation.

Ellen swallowed so that her voice would come out steady, because she discovered she was perilously close to tears. "Of course, I'll keep your secret. I'm—I'm not a—"

"A big mouth?" Dave supplied, his voice a little lighter. "I know. So we'll trust you. Believe me, Ellen, we're trusting you with a lot."

With a swift gesture, Debbie squeezed Ellen's arm close to her and leaned to give Ellen a light kiss on her cheek.

"I *am* glad you know," Debbie said. "It will be wonderful to have another girl to talk to, even if we don't get to see each other often."

Ellen's smile came then. "I think it's really neat," she said breathlessly. "I mean, I think it's the most exciting thing in the whole world."

Dave suddenly hugged her hard. "You're a good kid, Ellie," he said. He had never used the nickname before. "When Debbie and I get married, you can be maid of honor. Now, how about heading back to the crowd and letting us become as inconspicuous as possible?"

"Okay!" With an awkward wave of her mittened hand, Ellen turned and ran. She sensed, rather than saw, that the shadows behind merged again and then drifted apart, each going to an opposite side of the crowd.

The game was over by the time she got back to the rink, and Aunt Betty's team had won. So Ellen was caught up in the congratulations, and there was no time for her to think of what had happened out under the tree.

It was only later, after she was warm in bed, that her mind had time to sort out the events of the day. She remembered what Dave had said about the little deer, about Pete Wawaskesh, and she remembered the jerk of her heart seeing Debbie in

Dave's arms.

Something's wrong, Ellen said to herself. *Something's terribly wrong. Otherwise, why doesn't Dave date Debbie openly? Is it because of Patty? Does Debbie's grandfather forbid her to date? But he likes Dave. It must be something else.*

A dim little thought nibbled at the edges of her mind, the thought that maybe the disapproval came from a different direction altogether. But she turned her back on the thought. She opened her eyes and stared at the small, dim silhouette of the deer against the snow. A feeling of peace came to her then, a feeling that it would be all right. She had only to wait and keep quiet, and everything would be all right.

11

Valentine's Day, after the monotony of weeks of winter, was a little like a pink rose in a plain vase. There wasn't much said or done about it in school, but there was a large package of Ellen's favorite chocolates from her father and Frances, several pretty cards, and a pink frosted cake in the shape of a heart furnished by Aunt Betty, who seemed to know that Ellen was going through a rough time. And most exciting of all, there was a Valentine card—a most unexpected Valentine card—from a boy!

Ellen never even thought of Steve Upton on that particular day. After that talk with Mary Ann, she had written to her father and asked if Steve still lived at the apartment house. Daddy had written that he did and sometimes asked about her, and after this Ellen had more or less stopped thinking about him. The inquiry to her father had just come from the fact that she and Mary Ann had been talking about boys, but she certainly hadn't gone back to that giddy feeling she had a year ago that made her think a miracle had happened if Steve even looked at her.

So it was a bolt out of the blue to find a card on her dresser after school with the rest of the mail, a card addressed in boyish writing that was not immediately recognizable. She opened it up and gazed in complete astonishment at the scrawled note on the back. The verse was not sentimental—just friendly—but the written words were exciting, the more so because they were really unexpected.

"Dear Ellen," Steve wrote. "I thought about you when I was looking for a card for my mother, so I thought I'd send you one, too. Hope you're having a great winter. Things are just the same here. We've been enjoying some good movies, and there have been a couple of pretty good parties. If you want, I'd like to write to you. Your friend, Steve. P.S. I see your dad quite often. He says you're coming home for Easter. I'll see you then."

Wow! thought Ellen. *Who would ever think he'd send me a card?*

Her eyes were sparkling as she set the card on the dresser. Mary Ann and Debbie weren't the only ones who would get Valentines. It was a lovely feeling!

Sam managed to spoil it just a little for her later that evening. He started to tease her about having a boyfriend, and she realized almost at once that he must have gone into her room and looked on her dresser. How else would he have known? She felt again the touch of anger that Sam sometimes aroused in her. He had no right, absolutely no right, to go into her room. It was on the tip of her tongue to tell him so when she remembered that, in reality, it was Sam's room, not hers. In spite of all the warmth shown to her by everyone else, there was still this awareness that Sam had not wholly forgiven her for taking his room. Maybe he felt he had a right to step into it, to look around.

But not to read my private mail, Ellen thought bitterly, holding her lips tightly together. She wondered, then, how many other private things he had seen, had looked into. She would have to be careful from now on. She would even have to be careful about what she wrote to her father. It was not a comfortable feeling at all.

She waited a week or two before she wrote to Steve. She didn't want to seem too eager. But then she wrote and told about the island and the school and all the things that were lovely and good. She did not tell of the boredom that had touched her so frighteningly at times during the long, long winter. She did not mention the fact that she was beginning to suspect that she was still a stranger who did not really understand the true feelings on the island. She had been so sure, so completely sure, that the islanders felt as she did about the Indians. But the mystery of Dave's and Debbie's relationship had started to shake her confidence in her own beliefs, and she did not want to give those feelings the reality of words on paper.

Steve answered, and several letters were exchanged between Valentine's Day and Easter. Through their correspondence Ellen discovered that he was even nicer than she remembered. Last year, she had been silly and thirteen years old, and she had only noticed that he had blue eyes and was tall and good-looking. Now she was discovering that he was intelligent and sensitive and had a sense of humor. It wasn't like falling in love with him all over again. It was something quite different, and she didn't even try to understand it.

Letters came from daddy, too, and from Frances. They told her of their wedding plans, and they asked her if she would be the maid of honor. The day that particular letter came, she went to Aunt Betty.

"I need advice," Ellen confessed candidly.

Aunt Betty, in her calm, unruffled fashion, didn't even answer until she had poured a glass of milk for

Ellen and a cup of coffee for herself. She took some freshly baked cookies out of a jar and put everything on the little table that looked out over the ice-locked bay.

When Aunt Betty spoke, her voice was gentle. "What about? Or can I guess?"

Ellen looked at her, wondering if she could possibly put it into words.

"It's about the wedding," she said.

"And you're wondering if you'll be unfaithful to the memory of your mother if you take part in it?" Aunt Betty asked.

Ellen nodded, not even wondering how Aunt Betty knew.

Aunt Betty was silent for another minute, sipping her coffee and gazing out the window.

"You know, Ellen, there's no easy answer for that. I mean, I can only tell you how *I* feel. I can't tell *you* how to feel."

"I know," Ellen said, "but maybe I can think clearer if I know how *you* feel."

"I loved your mother very much," Aunt Betty said. "I suppose I'll miss her till I die. But I have my family—and even you for now—and your dad doesn't have anyone. I don't think your mother would want him to be lonely."

"Oh, I know that," Ellen said. "I don't want him lonely either. But they want me to be the maid of honor. Would that be wrong?"

Aunt Betty shook her head. "No, not wrong.

Your whole loyalty lies, or should lie, with your father. If taking part in his wedding makes him happy, then that's all that should matter."

Ellen was silent, thinking. She really hadn't stopped to think that what she did or didn't do about this request would affect her father's happines.

"Of course," Aunt Betty went on, "it would be wrong if you felt guilty or bitter about it. If you stood beside Frances at the altar with a frozen face and resentment in your heart, then they'd be better off having you just sitting with the other guests, or even staying here."

Those were blunt words, indeed, and Ellen sat for a long time in total silence, tumbling the words over and over in her head. *Was* she grown up enough to be really happy for her father and Frances and not just put on an act?

"Tell me about Frances," Aunt Betty said casually. "You know, I've never met her."

Ellen groped for words. "She's—well, she's not as pretty as my mother—and you. She's short and slim, and she has dark hair. She laughs a lot. I mean she's not silly, but it's as though she were happy. She doesn't act—well, romantic around my dad, but she acts as though—I don't know how to say it—as though he makes her comfortable and happy. He does, too. Act that way, I mean.

Aunt Betty was silent and Ellen slid a look at her. "She sounds nice, doesn't she?" Ellen said at last.

Aunt Betty nodded, and her smile was warm.

"So if I kicked up a fuss or acted stuffy, I'd only be selfish. I wouldn't really be thinking of mom at all, but only of me. Is that what you wanted me to discover?"

"I hoped you would discover it," Aunt Betty said. "I'm not saying it'll be easy. But I think it's something you could do."

Ellen nodded decisively. "I'll write to them right away," she said. She got up quickly from the table. "If you don't mind, I'll go write the letter now."

"No better time," said Aunt Betty serenely.

Ellen paused at the door and looked back at her aunt. "What do you suppose I'll wear?" she said.

The weeks moved faster after that. There was something to look forward to, something different. Word came from Washington that Ellen was to wear a long dress, very old-fashioned looking, with puffy sleeves and a high neck, and she would carry a colonial nosegay of daisies and rosebuds. There was a swatch of the material enclosed, and it was a sort of sprigged dimity, predominately pink, feminine, and delicate. It was enough to make any girl start to get really excited, and letters full of plans flew back and forth constantly.

The wedding was to be the day after Easter, so they decided that Ellen would leave Sudbury on the Thursday before Easter so she'd have a few days at home. Then, she and her father and Frances would fly to Toronto together the day after the wedding. The honeymooners would stay in Toronto for a week, and Ellen would fly directly back to Sudbury. Unfortunately, it would be a short visit, but she really didn't dare take any more time away from school.

During the weeks of waiting, two things happened that caused Ellen to do a lot of thinking.

The first thing was a conversation she had with Rachael. On a bright, cold Saturday they had gone to West Bay with Mr. Enoss. While they were waiting for him to finish his business, Rachael took Ellen to see the church that had been built to symbolize an Indian teepee. Although she had ridden by it many times, Ellen had never been inside before, and she was fascinated with the unusual, stylized interior.

"It's to represent a council meeting," Rachael explained. "See, no pews, just steps, like, in a circle, and the altar is where the fire would have been."

Ellen gazed around her in delight. The vivid designs behind the altar glowed in the dusky room, and the traditional, formalized carving of an eagle below the central roof opening was obviously an Indianized symbol for the Holy Spirit.

"Neat!" Ellen said. Then, cautiously, "Do only Indians belong here?"

"I guess so." Rachael's reply was careless.

"Doesn't it make you mad?" Ellen asked, her old grievances surging up in a bitter wave.

"Mad? Why?"

"That the Christian church—the place that should represent brotherhood and love—only separates people."

Rachael shook her head. "The church isn't to blame. It's people, maybe only a few people. You can't dump all the blame on the church. That's a cop-out!"

Just then, Mr. Enoss called to them from the front door, so they had to leave, and somehow they never got back to the conversation. Ellen didn't forget it, though. Rachael's comment had made Ellen's own criticism to her father seem childish and unreasonable. She didn't make any sudden decisions or even comment on it in her letters to her father, but about every other Sunday she started getting up to go to church with Aunt Betty. It was almost embarrassing how quickly she lost her prickly feelings and began to feel as though she had come home.

The second event that set her thoughts racing and tumbling was the meeting she had with Debbie in the art room. Ellen had come in to pick up some paper she had left there the day before, and Debbie was back in the corner working on a large oil painting that was usually kept in the cupboard.

Ellen stopped just inside the door, hesitating to come in, because if this were the exhibit, Debbie might not want anyone to see it.

Debbie looked up and smiled. "Hi," she said. "Come on in."

"Sure you don't mind?"

"Not if it's you. I wouldn't want just anyone peering over my shoulder."

Ellen moved with eager curiosity to the back of the room. She came to a stop behind Debbie and stood quietly looking at the painting. It was a woods scene, probably early spring, with bare branches and shady patches of snow. But there was a hint of green here and there, a proof that winter was past. Back in the trees, half hidden by a dark evergreen, a deer stood, poised for flight, head high, ears pricked forward. Ellen saw the same pure delicacy in the animal that was in her little carving.

"The blessing deer," Ellen said in a breathless way.

Debbie looked at her. "Dave's right," she said. "You do see a lot. You didn't learn that in *this* place."

Ellen gazed at her in shock. "What do you mean?" she said. "This would be the kind of place where a person *would* be most apt to—to 'see' things, as you and Dave say."

Debbie smiled. "You'd think so, wouldn't you? I've promised Dave I won't say—well, say wrong things to you. You're such a dreamer, Ellen. I thought all Yankees were greedy, selfish clods."

Ellen stared at her. "All Yankees aren't anything," she said flatly. "Any more than all Indians are or all Canadians. You know that, Debbie. You couldn't—you couldn't love Dave and not know that."

Debbie looked a little ashamed. "I'm only teasing," she said. "You're a doll and the best thing that has happened to this place in a long time."

Just then someone else came to the door and Debbie began to take her painting off the easel. Just before she moved away with it, Ellen saw what she hadn't seen before. The thing that had startled the deer was a boy standing off to one side, so blended into the tree trunks that he was nearly invisible. It was Dave, there could be no mistaking that. Only he was dressed in the old-time Indian clothing, shirt and leggings of some kind of skin and soft moccasins.

Ellen had no time to examine it, no time to ask about the boy, and the minute of privacy had given her nothing but more questions in her mind. And the questions kept recurring in the following days. Had Debbie dressed Dave like that because she thought of him that way? Or to disguise him? Or because she wished he was—what? An Indian?

I wish I didn't "see so much," Ellen thought miserably. *I wish I were like Mary Ann, or even dumb old Sam, and just saw what was obvious and didn't let it eat at me. I wish I—but daddy had said one time that to deny one's own personality was wrong. I just wish life was easier, or else that I was smarter or tougher.*

Easter came early in April that year, and the snow was perceptibly less deep than it had been in January, but there were really not many other signs of spring. The lake was still frozen, although Dave claimed the ice was softening. So it seemed really ridiculous for Ellen to pack spring clothes to take to Washington, even though Frances had written that they were having an early spring and with any luck they might have a lovely week for her.

Dave and Aunt Betty took her to Sudbury and put her on the plane. At the last minute Aunt Betty seemed reluctant to have her go. She hugged Ellen hard.

"Don't fall in love with the glamour of the city," she said. "We want you to come back, you know."

"You don't have to worry," Ellen said. "I'll be back in less than a week."

Dave grinned at her. "After a formal wedding and seeing your friend, Steve, Manitoulin is going to be pretty dull."

Ellen spoke quickly before her courage failed her. "No place in all the world would be dull if you were there, Dave."

He bent and kissed her cheek. "You are my idea of what all girls should be like," he said. "Observant and honest!"

It made it possible for them to leave each other

with laughter, and Ellen found that even when the plane was off the ground, she had no room for regret. She suddenly discovered that she was honestly as excited as she had been that long ago day in September when she had flown to the island in search of a dream.

The plane arrived in Washington right on time, in the hour before twilight blotted out the city. Ellen looked eagerly out of the window, not really sure what she was looking for. The tall, straight spire of the Washington Monument speared up into the sky to greet her, and there, very tiny and blurred, she caught a glimpse of the small, rounded dome of the Jefferson Memorial surrounded with—she hadn't even thought of it before—not snow or ice, but a white froth of blossom. The cherry trees were in bloom! It was like a miracle—blossoms and the swift glimpse of beauty in white buildings and grass that was already green. She hadn't expected this.

Even the crowded gloom of the National Airport failed to douse her enthusiasm. She came off the plane into an evening that was only a little chilly—not cold—and there, waiting for her, were her father and Frances, both of them looking a little scared.

She flew at them, some instinct making her throw her arms around Frances first and then turning to her father for his hug.

"Oh!" she said because there weren't any other words available. And the next words came out without her really knowing what she was going to say. "It's fabulous to get home!"

12

The first few hours in Washington were enough to make Ellen's head spin. She hadn't really thought she would be all that glad to get back. Oh, she knew she'd be happy to see her father, of course, and even glad to see Frances, and pleased to be in her own familiar room. But she certainly hadn't anticipated the flood of—what? It wasn't exactly happiness or joy or even pleasure, but a—she felt silly saying it to herself—a sort of coming back into herself when she walked in the door of her room. She knew, then, not clearly, perhaps, but in a vague sort of way, that her room on the island was still a *borrowed* room. It was

Sam's and all her delight over the ruffled spread and the lovely, lovely view from the window did not change that.

Here, there was quite a different view. Their apartment was on the side of the building that faced toward the center of Washington so that Ellen could see the Capitol from her window—with, of course, a hundred buildings between her and the gleaming dome. But she hardly saw the sprawl of buildings in her first viewing of the old familiar scene. She saw only the lighted gold dome against the April sky, and it was quite beautiful.

Once again the feeling filled her that belonging to two families, belonging to two places, was the most difficult thing in the world. It must be a bit like the lady in the circus who got sawed in half. She wondered fleetingly if she, like the circus lady, would come out whole and smiling. And what would she be? *Who* would she be?

But there was no time for speculation and dreaming and wondering. They went out to dinner, and Ellen discovered that it *was* fun to be in a room with gleaming silver and elegant decorations and food served in dishes that she wouldn't have to wash afterward.

But best of all was talking with her father and Frances. She had worried that maybe it would be awkward to be three when they had been two before, but she needn't have worried. Frances was so much like Ellen's father that they seemed to knit together in a comfortable way immediately.

"Will I try on my dress tomorrow for the wedding?" Ellen asked.

Frances nodded. "We'll go shopping in the morning so we can get that all taken care of. Then you can spend the afternoon looking up old friends or whatever you want. And I understand your evening is already spoken for."

Ellen looked inquiringly at her father.

"Stephen Upton," daddy explained. "He called a week or so ago and said he'd like to take you to a play. I said you could let him know late tonight, but I have a sneaking suspicion that he got the tickets just in case."

Ellen's eyes got round. "Wow," she breathed, "a real date. I never had one before. Not that kind."

"Of course, you're much too young," her father began, but he was smiling and Frances interrupted.

"Too young for lots of things, perhaps, but not too young for a date to a play on a brief visit to the city."

"Right!" Ellen said and grinned at both of them.

She called Steve as soon as they got back to the apartment, and she felt shy and awkward when she heard his voice.

"This is Ellen Ramsey," she said.

"Oh, hi," he answered, and then there was a long pause and she had a terrible feeling that he was sorry she had called.

"Did I call too late?" she said. "I didn't know. My

father said I ought to call."

"Oh, no. It's just—I didn't know how to talk to someone who's been away for so long."

Ellen laughed. "I guess just the same as you used to."

"I didn't talk very much before. I'm not too good with girls," Steve confessed.

And all the time she had thought he was a snob, and here he was just scared like she sometimes was. Only now he was a year older.

"Anyhow," Steve went on with determination, "did your dad tell you I want to take you to the play tomorrow night?"

"Yes, he told me."

"Will you go?"

"I'd love to."

"Great! I'll pick you up about 7:30. My dad'll drive us over. Is that okay? We can get a cab to come home."

"Fine. That'll be fine," Ellen said, wondering whether she would really be able to stand all this and not just burst with the grown-up feeling that was filling her.

"Okay. See you. You can tell me all about Canada and everything. Bye."

"Bye." She hung up and turned to her father, who was watching her with no attempt to disguise his interest.

They had already taken Frances home because she said she had so much to do, but Ellen suspected that she was sensitive enough to know that Ellen would like to be with her father.

"How about that?" Ellen said. "We're coming home in a cab."

Mr. Ramsey sighed. "From one worry to another. When you're away I worry about boats and frostbite. When you're home, I worry about boys and crazy cab drivers."

"Don't worry," Ellen said comfortingly. "It'll only make you bald. Daddy, are you too tired to talk?"

"Never," he said. "Why don't you put on your pajamas and a robe, and I'll take off my coat and tie and we'll get comfortable and really make up for lost time."

They had always talked together, but there had never been a talk like this one. Here, in her father's home, Ellen felt no hesitation to say some of the things that had seemed a disloyalty at Christmas on the island. She told him about all the things that had hurt her, all the things that had enriched her. She told in detail about the accident with Sam and Andy and saw the fear in her father's eyes.

"Sam isn't nearly as nasty now," she hurried to add. "I think he likes me a little better. But Sam's funny."

"Maybe he's jealous," daddy said.

"Jealous?" She stared at her father with amazement.

"That you're so obviously a really important

person to Dave, Andy, and Aunt Betty, especially. Even Mary Ann. Maybe he thinks you threaten his—his position in the house."

"I never thought of that," Ellen said slowly. "I just try to keep out of his way."

She did not add that Sam's lack of generosity prevented her from feeling totally at home on the island. If she put those feelings into words, it would start to form decisions, perhaps, that she was by no means ready to make.

She told the whole story of the blessing deer, and she brought it out of her suitcase for her father to see again. He admired it as he had at Christmas and asked her several questions that led, even though she had not really meant to tell, to a discussion of Dave and Debbie.

"I just don't understand why they keep it so secret," she finished with misery. "I can't understand it."

"Maybe there are lots of people there who wouldn't approve of a white boy falling in love with an Indian girl," daddy said.

Those were the words Ellen had refused to even let come into her own mind, and she didn't want to hear them from her father. But at least he didn't just laugh and say that Dave and Debbie were kids, so what difference did it make.

Ellen shook her head stubbornly. "I can't believe that. I *won't*. There might be prejudice against some of the Indians; some of them aren't—well, very ambitious. But Debbie is just gorgeous. And smart. Aunt Betty and Uncle Archie couldn't object to *her*."

Her father started to say something and then changed his mind and, to Ellen's intense relief, asked something else that led the conversation into more comfortable areas.

She could see that he had made up his mind not to question her about church, so it took a little courage to admit to him that Rachael's realistic and grown-up attitude had shaken her old convictions.

"I'm not a gung-ho church person yet," she explained. "Not the way you are, not the way I used to be. But I'm going pretty often now. I—I think I've learned that the church isn't going to change if people just stop going. It's the people who have to change first. So if I really think I'm right, then I have to stay and fight for what I believe."

Mr. Ramsey's eyes shone. "You already know something many people never learn in a lifetime," he said. "I'm not going to worry about you anymore."

The talk went on and on until they both were staggering with weariness when they went to bed at 3:00 A.M. But Ellen felt as though she had shared so much of her Manitoulin experiences with her father that she really had not been away from him at all. It was a lovely feeling.

The shopping trip next morning was fun, and

Ellen and Frances had lunch in a small restaurant where they talked about how beautifully Ellen's dress had fit and all of the other exciting female things that go into a wedding.

After lunch, Frances dropped Ellen off, and Ellen went up to the apartment to leave her packages and wash her face. She had put off thinking about what she was going to do during the afternoon, not allowing herself to make definite plans. And yet, deep inside her heart, she knew all the time what she was going to do. Clarisse did not know she was home—daddy had said he hadn't seen her for weeks—and Ellen wanted to just walk into Clarisse's place and see how she'd act. If she acted like she did last fall, well, then that's how it was. Ellen would just accept it once and for all. But maybe, just maybe—

It was the "maybe" that took Ellen down the elevator and through the streets—marveling at the cool, delicate April sunshine—to the street where Clarisse's apartment was. As Ellen turned the last corner, her heart nearly jumped out of her chest because there, on the front stoop, sitting by herself, was Clarisse. She was sitting as Ellen had seen her sitting a hundred times; her knees drawn up under her chin; her arms wrapped around her legs; her chin propped on her arms. She even had on the red slacks and sweater Ellen had helped her pick out last summer, and for just a second Ellen thought she couldn't stand it. Nothing else was as critical as this minute—not the meeting at the airport, or trying on the maid of honor dress, or talking to Stephen on the phone. For a few seconds Ellen stood in absolute silence, trying to steady her racing heart. Then she began to walk slowly along the sidewalk.

Clarisse didn't look up, and finally Ellen called to her in a voice that shook badly. "Clarisse! Hey, I'm home."

Clarisse looked up, and her face was flooded with total amazement and disbelief. And then in a flash, she was off the porch and racing down the sidewalk toward Ellen, her arms opened wide. They met with a hug that was so fierce that it nearly knocked them both over.

"I don't believe it," Clarisse kept saying. "I don't believe it."

"You aren't mad at me anymore," Ellen said, which was probably the dumbest, most childish thing she had ever said in her whole life, she thought despairingly.

"I was weird," Clarisse said. "Don't pay any attention to what I did back then. Randy got to me a lot, and I did some weird things."

Ellen felt as though her face would stretch out of shape if she didn't quit grinning so idiotically.

"Oh, I'm so glad to see you," Ellen said.

"Me, too. You're the only girl in the whole class who knows me from nothing," Clarisse said. "Are you back to stay?"

"No. Only five days."

"Are you going to live on the island forever?" Clarisse asked. "I mean, isn't it dead up there in the woods? I suppose the people are wonderful and all, but still—"

Ellen laughed. "There are parts of it that are so great you wouldn't believe it. But I haven't decided yet. It's hard to know what to do. If you could see how beautiful it is, or if you could meet Dave, or—"

Nothing had changed. They talked without stopping for the entire afternoon. Ellen discovered with disappointment that Clarisse's current attitude toward Ellen did not include other white girls. There was still bitterness and frustration and resentment. The real change was that somehow Clarisse had discovered during the winter that Ellen was a person, not just a white girl.

Randy came in while they were talking, and the look he shot at Clarisse was not a warm one. But he was civil to Ellen, which was all she could really hope for.

After he left, Clarisse was quite candid. "Randy really got me all uptight last summer. He made me believe that every white person in the world was my enemy. He's still right about some things, but I'm learning to think for myself. We do get a rotten deal here—worse than anywhere else, I guess—but my getting mad at you was stupid."

"I wish you could come to the island," Ellen said. "It's so different there."

"Really?" Clarisse said eagerly. "Are people *really* different?"

"Oh, yes," Ellen said. Then she added honestly, "Or most of them are. They really are."

Clarisse shrugged. "I guess it doesn't make any difference to me, anyhow. My folks aren't likely to leave Washington, and it'll be a long time until I'm old enough to go where I want to go. So, I just make the best of it. At least I'm not as uptight as Randy. That's something."

After the reunion with Clarisse, Ellen was afraid that the date with Steve would be slightly anticlimactic. But the play was wonderful, and Steve was fun to be with—after he got over his first shyness. Ellen found she could talk to him about lots of things she had never dreamed she could talk about to a boy. She even told him about Clarisse.

"Clarisse is funny," Steve said. "I'm glad she smartened up about you. She's been lonely since you left, but I was afraid she'd be too stubborn to figure out why. She's really rotten to lots of the white kids."

"They're rotten to her," Ellen said defensively.

"Sure, I know. But not all of them. She won't even let people be friendly lots of times".

"It's different when you're black," Ellen said.

"Or pink or purple," Steve said. "But people can't help being different. And prejudice is kind of normal, isn't it?"

"No, not really. White people up on the island aren't prejudiced."

"Honest?" He looked impressed.

"Well, not the ones I know," she said a little feebly.

He shrugged. "See? The people you know here aren't prejudiced either. You aren't the kind of girl who would be friends with dumb people who call other people names and things like that."

She looked at him, aware of the compliment in his words. She decided that if he kept on like this, by the time he got to be nineteen, he'd *really* be as nice as Dave.

When he said good night to her at her door, he turned shy again. "You won't have time to see me anymore this visit, will you?" he said.

She shook her head regretfully. "We have so much to do and only a couple of days."

"I know. Are you coming back this summer?"

"Oh, sure. Sometime."

"To stay?" he asked.

"I don't know," she said. "I really don't, Steve. Everything has been so wonderful this visit, but I remember the bad and ugly things, too. And the island—well, it's so fabulous I'm not sure I could leave it."

Steve smiled. "Maybe you'll change your mind, too," he said. "I'll write if you'll answer."

She nodded her head yes, and he bent down quickly and kissed her, an awkward, sweet kiss that landed on the corner of her mouth. It was her first kiss and she was suddenly glad that it had come like this, and not in some foolish game or silly kid-fooling around.

"Good-bye, Steve," she said.

"Good night, Ellen," he said.

She watched him walk down the hall and then opened her door and went inside, aware of a feeling inside her that was an odd mixture of happiness and a sadness that was almost pain.

The wedding was beautiful! Ellen's fears that she would disgrace her father and cry were completely unfounded. She discovered that there was only contentment in her heart, along with a big measure of excitement over being an honest-to-goodness maid of honor and wearing such a gorgeous dress. She never fumbled when she handed over the ring, and her eyes met Frances's directly with so much warmth that Frances looked suddenly radiant. Seeing her gladness, Ellen was ashamed that she had ever hesitated at all.

There were only a few guests and the reception was small, but the entire time was happy, laced with laughter and joy. Ellen was allowed her first taste of caviar, and that was her only disappointment. She had expected it to taste absolutely elegant, but it tasted like salty gelatin.

She wrinkled her nose in distaste and her father

laughed at her. "That's life," he said to her. "Especially for you. You're always expecting everything to be beautiful. And when it isn't, you're amazed."

He was right, and she knew it. But she also knew that the disappointing taste of caviar didn't spoil her pleasure with the reception anymore than Sam's behavior spoiled her love for the Ludlows. So that was *something* to be said in her favor, anyhow.

She spent that night with Clarisse—something she had thought she would never do again—and they talked most of the night. They didn't talk seriously, and there was still a faint distance between them. But they were both different, Ellen knew. They couldn't be separated for nearly eight months—both of them having totally different experiences—and come back and just pick up where they left off. There would have to be time to get reacquainted. But the bitterness was gone, and for now that was more than enough for Ellen.

In the morning, Clarisse said at the last minute, "I hope you come home to stay, Ellen. Randy would really get bent out of shape if he heard me say so, but I can't help it."

Ellen hugged her quickly. "Thanks," she said. "If I come home, you can be sure it'll be a lot because of you."

"I might get nasty again," Clarisse said soberly.

"I don't think I would, but I might."

Ellen smiled, "And I might bend *you* out of shape if you do."

The perfectly amazing thing was that at that minute they were closer than they had ever been, even during all the time when Ellen was being so compassionate because she thought she understood Clarisse's turning against her. Their last sentences had been completely honest, *and that is a good thing for friends to be,* Ellen thought.

Leaving Washington was different this time. It was both harder and easier. The newlyweds were so happy that Ellen was content to just bask in their glow. She had so much to think about, so many emotions to sort out, that she felt no jealousy at all over the fact that her father and Frances seemed completely absorbed in each other.

Even the parting in Toronto wasn't too sad because Ellen knew they'd all be together in the summer. Her father was going to bring Frances to the island and Ellen would be going to Washington, either for a month or for good. Just for this minute, she wouldn't let herself worry about which way it was going to be.

The closer the plane got to Sudbury, the more nervous Ellen got. Maybe, after her fabulous time at home, she might feel different about coming to Canada than she had felt last September.

And she did, but not at all in the way she had

anticipated. There was no nervousness in her this time, no strangeness, no wondering how it was all going to be. Now there was the safe, serene feeling of coming home. The Ludlows all looked beautiful to her, standing at the edge of the field—the snow had nearly all disappeared, she discovered—and she was as glad to see them as though she had been gone for a month.

It was on the way back to the island that they told her the tragic news. The ice had broken up, and four days ago old Pete Wawaskesh had taken his boat out as soon as he could get away from shore—a bad habit he had followed for years—and he had never come home. His boat had been found along the shore of one of the islands, and it looked as though it had been pulled up on shore, but there was no sign of Pete. The nights were still bitter, Aunt Betty said soberly, and in spite of the old fellow's skill in the woods, there was little hope for his survival, even though everyone was still searching for him.

Ellen shot a quick look at Dave and saw what she had failed to see in the gladness of the first greeting. He looked older and worried, and there were lines at the corner of his mouth.

What about Debbie? Ellen wanted to ask, but Dave's look at her was a warning one. The mystery still existed. As far as the Ludlows were concerned, old Pete's disappearance was a tragedy just because he was an old man whom they had all known through Dave.

No one said anything about Debbie, who was all alone now, Ellen thought. All alone except for Dave. And Dave was making no claim.

13

The disappearance of old Pete Wawaskesh was the main topic of conversation at school and at the Ludlow house for days after Ellen's return to the island. The search for the old man went on for about a week, but then it was given up on the assumption that he could not possibly still be alive in the unpredictable April weather. Although the ice had broken up rapidly and the snow had nearly all disappeared in the pale, uncertain sunshine of the early northern spring, there were still days of wind and blowing wet snow, and at night fresh thin ice formed at the shoreline and in the puddles in the lane.

Debbie stayed out of school for a week and then she came back, looking wan and thin with dark circles under her eyes, but with courage in her smile. She was staying with the Enosses temporarily, and Rachael told Ellen that she heard Debbie cry in the night sometimes but no one seemed to know how to comfort her.

Ellen watched Dave go around tight-lipped and silent until she finally couldn't stand it any longer. They had hardly had a chance to exchange a dozen words since Ellen's return, and there were things she felt she *had* to say to him. In spite of the difference in their ages, she felt absurdly maternal, and she was sure she could offer him comfort and advice.

So, taking all her courage in her hands, she knocked on Dave's door one afternoon late in April. It had been a windless day, not too cold, and she used the weather as an excuse.

"Dave," she called, "it's a nice day and I'm dying to take a walk, but Mary Ann's busy. Could—would you come with me?"

There was silence for a second, and she heard the springs creak on his bed as though he had turned over.

"It's muddy," he said.

"I know. But it's not cold and I'd love to get some fresh air."

Another brief hesitation and then he said, "Okay, just a second."

When he opened his door, she darted a quick look at him. He looked awful, really awful.

"I'm sorry," she said with contrition. "Were you sleeping?"

He laughed, a short, bitter sound. "Sleep? What's that?"

"Oh, Dave, I'm sorry. You don't have to go with me. I shouldn't have bothered you."

He managed to smile at her. "It'll do me good. Blow the cobwebs out of my head."

They walked in silence until they had reached the end of the muddy lane and turned onto a drier road that angled through the pine woods.

Finally Dave spoke, and Ellen could see that he had to make a real effort at conversation. It was as though his mind just plodded around in tight circles and could hardly take in anything else but the one thought that obsessed him.

"I haven't even asked you about your trip," he said, trying to make his voice casual. "Did you have a good time?"

Maybe if she talked as casually as he, the conversation would lead around to what she really wanted to say. It was worth trying.

"It was marvelous," she said. "I didn't expect it to be so great."

"Really approve of the marriage, do you?"

"Oh, yes. But that was only part of it. I—well, I made up with my best friend."

He slanted a look at her. "I never even knew

you'd had a fight."

"I couldn't talk about it," she said slowly. "It was too awful to talk about. We'd been best friends for three years, and then she—well, she got mad at me."

"Steal her boyfriend?"

How could he possibly know that it wasn't some silly thing like that at all? It was true she hadn't even mentioned Clarisse's name up here, but one of her reasons for coming to the island was to get away from the pain of Clarisse. Now, however, she could talk about it—now that everything was all right.

"Nothing like that," she said. "It was really awful. Clarisse's black, you see, and she got really all hung up over it and felt that even *I* had to be her enemy, just because I was white. I felt terrible."

They walked a minute or two in silence while Ellen tried to put her feelings into words that made sense. "When it happened, I forgave her for being rude and nasty and everything, because I thought she had a right to be like that. Black people really do have it rough at home. But I don't think I'd be so bighearted again. I think I'd tell her to shape-up. It wasn't *my* fault the slaves were brought to America."

"Nor mine that the Indians got shoved onto a reservation," Dave muttered.

"But that's different," Ellen cried. "You don't have the same kind of prejudice up here."

Dave kicked viciously at a root. "Ellen, when I realized you were so obviously starry-eyed idealistic about believing there was no prejudice on the island, I swore I'd keep my mouth shut. I wanted you to like us, to keep on believing we were as great as you thought we were. I figured you'd get your eyes opened in school, but I swear, you walk around in your own little cloud of goodness."

"Nuts!" said Ellen clearly, but she was remembering her father's comment after she had the caviar. Was it true that she really expected life to be beautiful and perfect and so, in a sense, closed her eyes to obvious faults?

"You do," Dave insisted. "There's probably as much prejudice against the Indians on Manitoulin as there is against the blacks in Washington."

"I don't believe it," Ellen said flatly.

"Oh, don't you? How many Indians have you seen dating white kids?"

"But what about Rachael?" Ellen cried. "What about you and Tom? What about you and Debbie?"

"Yeah," Dave said bitterly. "What about us? As for you and Rachael or me and Tom, that's different. No one cares about kids being friends. But dating—or falling in love—that's altogether different. Why do you think I hide the fact that I'm crazy about Debbie?"

"I don't know," Ellen said miserably. "Maybe because of Patty."

"Nuts to Patty," Dave exploded rudely. "I don't care anything about her. She only likes me because she knows I'm not interested. No, I hide it because everyone would make Debbie's life miserable if it got out that she was going with a white guy."

"I don't believe it," Ellen said again, stupidly, but they were the only words she could think of.

"You don't have to believe it," Dave said, "but that doesn't change the fact that it's true. If you were to ask an islander if he were prejudiced against Indians, he'd say, 'Of course not. I've known lots of honest Indians.' "

"Dave, they wouldn't!"

"They have and they do and they will. Oh, not all of them, of course. We have decent, kind people here like everywhere else. And even the ones who are prejudiced don't think they are."

Ellen was silent, but her dreams were tumbling down around her ears. She had come here to find the tolerance and love that she had believed would be the natural outgrowth of the serene loveliness of the island, and Dave was ruthlessly stripping away her illusions.

"It's not all the fault of the white folks," Dave said soberly. "Some of the Indians are dirty and lazy and shiftless. But some of them are proud and good and smart. Only, no one gives them a chance. The reservation is just another kind of ghetto, you know."

"But it's so nice at Rachael's," Ellen protested.

Dave shrugged. "Sure, it's nice. Mrs. Enoss is as good a housekeeper as you'd find on the island, but you don't see any of the white women making friends with her."

"But what about Debbie?" Ellen said at last. "Now that old Pete's gone, what's going to happen to her?"

"Miss Numadabi's getting her a scholarship," Dave said. "She's been working on it all year. She'll go to school down in Toronto in June—start in summer session. I think I'm going to go to school there, too. When we're off the island, when we're in a city where people are more—what's the word, cosmopolitan?—we can start to go together openly."

"Big deal," Ellen said, suddenly angry. She had never dreamed she could be angry with Dave. "So for another month and a half she has to be lonely and alone because you're afraid to admit she's your girl. It wasn't so bad when her grandfather was alive. She had someone then. But who does she have now? You ought to do something!"

The words hung in the air like floating pellets of bitterness, and Ellen walked in tight misery. Whatever had given her the right to say such brutal things to Dave? What was she thinking of?

"I notice that when your friend got mad at you, all *you* could think of was running away where no one could hurt you," Dave responded in a very quiet voice that cut like steel.

She deserved that, but for a minute she thought she absolutely couldn't stand it.

Dave spoke in a toneless voice. "I'm sorry, Ellen. I shouldn't have said that."

"I'm sorry, too," she whispered. "I was awful. And you've been so good to me ever since I came. I had no right—"

"It's okay," he said, interrupting her. "We both—"

"We both were honest," Ellen said, interrupting him in turn. "And we can't take it. As long as we're polite, it doesn't matter how phony we are."

Dave reached over and squeezed her hand. "It's just that I don't know what to do. I'm half out of my mind with worry. I can't stand it if Debbie's hurt, hurt more than she has been, I mean. And I'm scared to death someone will find old Pete."

Ellen stared at him in astonishment. "What do you mean? Of course you want someone to find him."

Dave was quiet, walking so rapidly that she had to almost run to catch up. Then he started to talk, cutting his words off sharply. "If anyone finds him, they'll bring him home to bury him. They'll lay him out in a casket and it'll be all wrong."

"Why?" Ellen asked. "At least Debbie will *know*."

"Debbie knows now," Dave said. "She knows he's dead, and she can stand that because he was an old man and he was starting to forget and he wasn't himself anymore. Dying isn't so terrible when you're that old. And Pete wanted to die alone in the woods, in his own way."

"You mean, you mean he killed himself?"

"No! No, I'm sure he died accidentally. But it was the way he would have wanted it. He told me so lots of times. Debbie, too. *I'm* the one who's got to find him, so he can stay in the woods he loved."

Dave sounded almost embarrassed when he spoke those last words; he thought she might laugh at him.

"Couldn't you just *tell* people?" Ellen asked. "Tell them that Pete—"

"Ellen, try to get it through your head that people wouldn't understand."

"*I* can understand," Ellen said stubbornly. "I feel something about the little blessing deer. Other people might, too."

Dave turned on her in exasperation. "If you have any feeling for Debbie at all, you'll just keep your mouth shut about the whole thing. Let her work it out in her own way. We can manage."

Ellen stood in the middle of the road staring at her tall cousin. It was bad enough that Dave had shown her that ugliness and intolerance were not limited to any geographical place. But far worse, he seemed perfectly willing to not only admit the existence of the hate but to accept it. He wasn't *doing* anything to change the situation.

She opened her mouth to say what she was

thinking when that one cruel statement of Dave's came into her mind again: "I notice that when your friend got mad at you, all *you* could think of was running away where no one could hurt you." And it was true. It was true! She and Dave were two of a kind—so good on the outside, but inside they weren't any better than anyone else.

Ellen turned with a sob and started to run back toward the farm.

"Wait," Dave called. "Wait, Ellen, I'm sorry."

But she wouldn't wait. She didn't understand anything anymore. There was nothing solid to hold onto or believe in. The island was no better than Washington, and Dave was no better than the weakest part of herself.

She ran and ran, her breath coming in sobbing gasps. She knew from the silence that Dave wasn't running after her, and she was torn between being grateful that he let her be alone and wishing that he would catch her and somehow make everything all right again.

14

Ellen learned more during the next two weeks than at any other time in her life. She learned that she could hide a heartache even when there were times she thought she couldn't stand it. And she learned the most important lesson of all—that life goes on in a steady, ordinary way even when dreams and plans and hopes are torn to shreds.

She learned the last lesson just by doing what had to be done. She went to school and helped Aunt Betty and talked to Mary Ann and worked on the paintings she was hoping would be included in the exhibit late in May. She discovered she could talk and smile and even laugh, and no one knew there was anything hurting her heart. She wrote cheerful letters to her father and Frances, and she watched spring start its fragile greening of the island. But at night, alone in her bed, she wept for the friendship she and Dave had shared, believing she had lost it forever. She tried to pray about it—not because she had promised her father—but because she had nowhere else to turn. But she didn't have the courage to ask God to give her something she didn't feel she deserved.

Then, on a sunny Saturday in May, Ellen came back from getting the mail and saw Dave down at the dock working with the boat. For just a second she thought longingly of how it used to be when there had been no bitter words between them and she would have run down to share whatever he was doing, instead of standing alone in the yard.

Just at that minute, Dave looked up and saw her. "Hey," he yelled. "Ask mom if you can come out with me. Grab some lunch in case we're gone for a while."

He was so casual that it was as though there had never been any anger between them, and her heart began to race as an absurd happiness filled her.

She turned to run toward the house and Dave called again. "Bring a scarf or parka—the flies might be bad."

In less than fifteen minutes she was back at the boat, the picnic box under her arm, her heart feeling as light and airy as a balloon. They started out, not talking about anything more important than keeping the food away from the gasoline can. And then, when they were safely out in the channel, Dave let the motor out, and they were skimming over the water, the breeze strong and clean and fresh in their faces.

At first Ellen was too shy to look at Dave, but when she finally glanced at him she discovered that he was watching her, grinning. It was the old grin, with no reserve in it, no holding back, no hidden anger.

"You can hate me forever if you want to," Dave said.

"I thought you hated me," she said.

"I almost did for a little while," he said soberly. "It's not nice to get a picture of yourself that you had managed to keep hidden for a long time, especially when it's a pretty rotten picture."

"Oh, David," she said, almost in a wail.

"It's okay, Ellie. I've been a clod and a heel and a couple of other things that I can't say in front of you. And I'm sorry. Forgive me?"

She looked at him, and he seemed to be dazzling in the sunlight. *I think I'd die for him,* she thought, *and I can't even tell him how to be happy with Debbie.*

"I forgive you," she said solemnly, because this wasn't something silly that could be tossed off lightly. "If you'll forgive me."

"I not only forgive you," he said, and this time he smiled at her, "but I also happen to love you, little cousin. I'll be grateful all my life that you came when you did. Because of you, I might be a real man someday.

She smiled with her whole heart showing. David had said he loved her. That was treasure enough to last for as long as memory lived.

They rode for a long time in silence, speaking only when it was necessary—to point out a loon or a leaping fish or a particularly lovely rock formation at the edge of one of the islands.

Ellen didn't pay any attention at first to the direction in which they were headed, but finally she realized where they were. This was the area in which old Pete Wawaskesh had disappeared. Was Dave going to search for him now, today, with her along? She had a quick feeling of revulsion, of fear. What would they do if, by some strange chance, they discovered the—the body?

She looked at Dave and he was watching her. It was uncanny, but she knew he had been almost reading her thoughts.

"You said *you* could understand, remember?" he said.

"But, Dave, what if we do find him? Wouldn't he— I mean, aren't dead people—?" She couldn't finish her questions, but the horror probably showed on her face.

"Listen, Ellen, nature just sort of takes care of things like that. Old Pete's been gone nearly two months. There are birds and animals that eat carrion. There wouldn't be anything left to be afraid of—anything that would be disgusting or ugly. You don't have to be afraid."

She nodded, willing to trust his judgment.

"Last night," Dave said, "I woke up and suddenly remembered an old cave Pete took me to years ago on that island. It's not much of a cave, but I'll bet he tried to reach it for shelter. I'm not sure I can find it, but I want to try."

She swallowed, and a little shine went out of the day. But she nodded again dutifully. "Okay," she said.

In a few minutes Dave had pulled the boat up onto a stony beach and fastened a rope to a large rock. They got out and stood for a few minutes in the bright stillness. In spite of the brisk breeze, the stones were warm from the sun, and the dark trees behind them formed a shelter.

"Might as well have our lunch now," Dave said. "It's past noon, and I'm hungry."

Ellen had thought that the idea of why they were on the island would put all desire for food out of her mind, but she found that the sight of the sandwiches and fruit in the box looked marvelously inviting.

They talked very little as they ate, but they both were contented and happy. Ellen found herself wishing that this were that happy Saturday in September when she had caught the huge fish and life on the island had seemed to be made up of only lovely things. But it wasn't September, it was May and they had come here to find an old man who had died, an old man who had carved her beautiful little deer even though they had never met.

"Penny for your thoughts," Dave said.

But she only shook her head, smiling a little. She couldn't express her feelings adequately, so it was better to just not say anything.

"I'm going to try to find the cave," Dave said. "Do you want to stay here? Maybe I was dumb to ask you to come."

"No. I want to come. I might—I might act like a baby if we find him. But I want to come."

"Okay. Let's go."

They walked around the shoreline for quite a long way, stepping carefully from stone to stone. The evergreens and the ground pine grew so close to the shore in places that they had difficulty getting past the growth, but they managed. At last, taking his sighting from another island that pushed above the water, Dave turned and struck inland. It was rough going, and there were times when Ellen wished she had stayed back on the shore by the boat and let Dave come alone.

She wasn't even sure what she was looking for. This didn't look like cave country. She finally said as much to Dave.

"It's not a cave exactly," he said. "Just rocks that come up and form a ledge. He could have crawled under it. He might even have been able to build a fire. It's not far now. You'll see the shelf of rocks. They kind of angle up like a rock slide."

Pine-tree branches tore at her hair and scarf, and the tip of one branch swept across her face with a sudden swish that nearly blinded her. She stopped, breathing hard, and stood quietly for a minute, rubbing at her eye where the branch had struck at her.

Blinking her eyes to clear them, she looked down at the ground and stared for a long minute at something that her eyes recognized but which her mind would not accept. It was a shoe, a man's shoe, turned grotesquely to one side but not fallen onto its sole as an empty shoe would have fallen.

"Dave," she cried, her voice coming out in a harsh squeak, "Dave, come quick. Oh, please hurry, please!"

She shut her eyes and stood swaying, sensing Dave's rush up to her, aware of his long silence, hearing the branches being shoved to one side, and the sharp indrawn sound of his breath. All the time she stood with her eyes shut, and in a minute she felt his hands leading her gently away and pushing her down on a warm, dry rock.

"You sit here," Dave said. His voice was husky and soft. "I'll hurry with what I have to do, and then we'll go back. Are you all right?"

"I'm all right," she whispered, but she didn't open her eyes and she sat in utter silence, hearing the sound of birds and wind as Dave worked to cover what they had found.

After what seemed like a very long time, Dave came to her and, taking her hands, pulled her up from the rock.

"Okay," he said. "Let's go. No one can find him; he's right where he'd want to be."

"Wait," she said. "Shouldn't we say a prayer at least?"

Dave looked embarrassed. "I don't think—" he began.

But she gathered up her courage. "I will." She had never talked to Dave about faith or prayer, but she knew what she had to do. She bowed her head and she felt Dave's stillness.

"Dear God," she said slowly, groping for the words, "we know that Pete's spirit isn't here. But he loved these woods so much that maybe it's right for his body to be here. So bless this place, Lord, and bless Debbie and Dave. And old Pete."

She didn't know quite how to end and then suddenly the words were there, remembered from a poem she and Clarisse had loved.

"Go, play with your towns you have
built of blocks,
Your towns where you would have
bound me.
I lie in my earth like a tired fox,
And my buffalo have found me."*

A silence stretched between them, and then

*Stephen Vincent Binet, "Ballad of William Sycamore."

188

Dave spoke huskily. "Thanks," he said, "that was perfect. Come on. We can leave him now."

Ellen felt weak and wobbly and she clung to Dave's hand as though she couldn't see the way to go. They walked in complete silence, struggling over the rough ground, pushing back the heavy branches, stumbling occasionally on protruding roots of trees. The going was a little easier around the shore, and finally they arrived at the little cove where the boat was beached, where only a few hours before they had sat and eaten in such safe normalcy.

At last, Ellen spoke. "Was he—could you tell—I mean how did it happen?"

"His pants leg was slit—by his knife, I think, and it's clear that the bones—well, he must have fallen and broken his leg. Somehow he dragged himself to that spot, heading for the cave, as I thought. Only he didn't quite make it. I don't think he suffered much. He was sort of sitting up. It was exposure that killed him. But he kept himself busy for a while."

Dave extended his hand and on the palm of it, glowing softly in the sunlight, was a nearly completed replica of Ellen's blessing deer. Beside it lay old Pete's knife.

"Oh, Dave," Ellen said, "it's your deer. He made it for you."

"My blessing deer," Dave said and gently put it in his pocket.

"Come on, Ellen, let's go home."

Dave took Ellen with him that night when he drove down to the reservation. She thought at first that he was using her as an excuse to go to Enosses, but he corrected that impression almost at once.

"I want you to be with me when I tell Debbie," he said. "She might need a girl. Men are sometimes pretty dumb about things like this."

He's wrong, Ellen thought. *Debbie wouldn't want anyone but him.* But she didn't say it. She was both humble and proud over his confidence in her.

When they got to the Enosses, Ellen went in and asked if Debbie could come out to the car for a minute. Rachael looked round-eyed with curiosity, but Ellen only made a little motion to her that tried to say everything would be explained later. Then she followed Debbie to the car and stood awkwardly while Debbie crawled in beside Dave.

Dave leaned across Debbie. "Come on, Ellie. Get in here with us."

Ellen got in and closed the door, and for a minute there was an odd, expectant silence. Dave put his arm around Debbie, and for a second she looked around to see if they were being observed and then, oddly enough, seemed to trust him enough to relax and lean against him.

"You found my grandfather, didn't you?" Debbie said, her voice very soft.

"Yes," Dave said.

"Tell me about it." Her voice was steady, but Ellen was aware of a trembling in the slight body next to her.

Dave told her everything, telling it all in a gentle, soft voice, holding her in his arm as he talked. He finished by showing her the little deer, and Ellen watched Debbie take the tiny animal in her slim, dark hands.

"It's not quite finished," she said, in a softly breaking voice.

"Neither am I," Dave said. "I have a long way to go before I become a real man but, because of you and Ellen here, I'm at least starting to grow up."

They looked at him, puzzled, uncertain what he meant.

"I'll be right back," he said and got out of the car and walked into the Enosses' house.

"What's he doing?" Debbie asked.

"I don't know," Ellen said.

They waited in silence and in a minute, Dave was back.

"I asked Mrs. Enoss if I could take you for a ride," he said to Debbie.

Her mouth flew open in startled protest, and he put the palm of his hand gently across it.

"Trust me, Debbie. If you can trust me to leave your grandfather in the woods where he'd want to be, you can trust me with this too."

Debbie spoke in a voice so soft that it was like a

dry leaf blowing. "You're too sensitive to be a white man," she said.

The silence crashed in the car. Dave pulled back and even in the dim light Ellen could see his face turn white.

"Debbie," Ellen cried, "what a perfectly awful thing to say!" She couldn't help herself. She had been through too much, had endured too much, had seen too much of intolerance and prejudice to bear a single bit more.

Debbie burst into tears and threw her arms around Dave's neck. "I didn't realize," she sobbed. "I didn't know how awful that would sound. I'm as prejudiced as everyone else and I thought I was the only one who was right. Oh, David, David, help me."

Ellen couldn't hear what he said, but she knew that this was a pain that could be healed only by these two—if, that is, it could ever be completely healed at all.

15

When Debbie had finally finished crying and Dave seemed calm again, they started to drive away from the reservation. There was no attempt at easy, casual chatter. All three of them had touched too much harsh reality that evening to come back easily to ordinary living. Ellen couldn't know at all what Dave and Debbie were thinking, but she was terribly aware of the tumbling of her own thoughts.

She was beginning to realize, as the car sped up the dark road of the island, that Dave had done a very courageous thing back there at the Enosses. He had been open and honest at last. Ellen wondered if what she had said to him that day in the pine woods had some bearing on what he had done. Maybe *that's* what he meant when he said that because of her he would be a man someday.

Ellen discovered that her hands were clasped so tightly together that her fingers ached. But she didn't loosen them, because she knew that her hands, like her heart, were in an attitude of prayer. And, for once, her prayers had nothing to do with herself. *Please,* she prayed with great intensity, *please make them brave enough, God. Give them all the love they'll ever need. O please, Lord, help them both. They're going to need all the help they can get.*

All at once, Ellen realized that they had turned onto the road that led to the farm, and the car was bucketing over the familiar spring ruts. She darted a quick glance over at Debbie to see that she, too, was aware of where she was and was staring at Dave in dismay.

"Where are we going?" Debbie asked, her voice faint and trembling.

"Home," said Dave briefly, "and, as Ellie pointed out to me, it's about time!"

Debbie looked at Ellen with questioning in her eyes, and then she turned back to Dave. "Oh, Dave," she wailed, "you know we've talked it all over. It won't help anything. Your folks will only be hurt. And I look awful."

"You couldn't look awful if you worked at it," Dave said shortly. "And my folks are just going to have to get used to it."

Ellen's heart was pounding so hard she felt as though her whole body was shaking. She had been so sure of herself that day in the woods, so glib and easy with the words she had hurled at Dave, so scornful of the fact that he wasn't doing anything to change the situation. Now, she discovered, she was scared to death, absolutely scared to death, and she wished with all her heart that she had kept her mouth shut. What if Aunt Betty—oh, no, not Aunt Betty—but what if Uncle Archie—no, *he* wouldn't be unkind, would he? Then Sam, what if—oh, what if *any* of them were cold? Or even worse, what if they laughed at Dave and Debbie? She bit her lip and thought she would surely die if things went wrong. In a very real sense, she would be responsible.

They drove into the lane and parked behind the house.

Dave glanced over and grinned at Ellen. "Don't look," he said, but she had no time to turn away before she saw him draw Debbie into his arms and bend down to kiss her gently.

A small electric shock went through Ellen. Steve Upton's kiss had been sweet and something to be remembered always, but it bore absolutely no resemblance to this kiss between Dave and Debbie.

Dave led the way into the house. He walked proudly, Ellen saw, and his face was bright. This was the Dave she was used to—not the tight-lipped, frozen boy who had gone silently about the house since old Pete had disappeared.

"Mom, dad," Dave called.

"We're in here," Aunt Betty answered. "In front of the tv."

Dave, Debbie, and Ellen walked into the living room, the warm, bright, familiar room that Ellen had grown to know like a second skin. *What does it look like to Debbie?* she thought. *Or is she too scared to see anything but the people?* They were getting up from their chairs, honest surprise on their faces.

"Mom, dad," Dave said, "I thought it was about time I brought my girl home for you to get to know. You've maybe met her before, when she was little. I think her grandfather brought her one time when he came to get me, but you might not remember. This is Debbie Wawaskesh. Debbie, my mother and father."

The silence was too brief to even be called a silence at all. Aunt Betty moved forward quickly, her hands out. "Debbie, how nice to have you. I feel I know you because I've heard so much about you from so many people."

Her smile was warm and kind, and if there was any strain in her, she hid it very well. Ellen nearly burst with pride. Breeding showed, she thought, remembering words her mother had once said. In an emergency, breeding always showed.

Uncle Archie was only a fraction later. "Debbie, welcome. Come in and sit down. Sam, turn off the tv. Andy, up from that chair so Debbie can sit down. Phil, how about getting some pop to drink? Ellen, don't stand there like a stranger. Help Phil and Sam get the glasses out."

Of course, Uncle Archie was a shade too hearty. But only a shade. Debbie would notice it, but she wouldn't dare condemn. She had showed her own secret prejudices too plainly that night to be critical of anyone else.

They all sat down except for Ellen and Phil and Sam, who headed for the kitchen to follow Uncle Archie's orders. For a few seconds they worked in silence, and then Sam darted a quick look at Ellen.

"How long have you known about this?" he whispered.

"Since early February," Ellen said. "Why?"

Sam looked amazed. "You mean you knew and you didn't tell *anyone*?"

Ellen stared at him evenly. "I'm not a person who tells things that are supposed to be secret," she said. "And I don't have to be threatened to keep still, either."

The blow went home, and Sam's face showed it. "You mean you kept quiet before—about me—just because—because you wanted to, not because I threatened you?"

"I kept quiet for a lot of reasons," Ellen said, "none of them very nice. I wish I could say I did it because I→liked you. But I'm afraid that wouldn't be true. I didn't even *try* to like you."

Sam stared at her, and she reached out a hand to him, knowing with shame that she should have had the courage to do this a long time ago.

"It was wrong of me not to try," she went on bravely. "You had a right to be mad because I just barged in and took your room. I'd like to be your friend, Sam. Will you let me?"

Sam didn't answer for a long minute. Then abruptly, and to Ellen's total disbelief, he leaned forward and kissed her cheek.

"That's the kiss I should have given you last October," he said and then turned to carry a tray of glasses into the living room.

"Does that mean he'll be my friend?" Ellen said in a dazed voice.

Phil looked embarrassed. "Sam's weird," he said. "But I guess he's finally decided you're worth keeping."

Ellen just shook her head helplessly and turned to get cookies out of the jar.

In that instant, a thought hit her so hard that she stopped with her hand in midair. In all the months she had been asking God to make Sam into a friend, she had never once considered asking God to let her become a friend Sam could like. How marvelous that God had answered the prayer she should have been praying—even before she had the sense to pray it.

She grinned so rapturously at Phil that he looked a little nervous.

"Don't worry, I'm okay," she hastened to add and then tried to bring her thoughts back to Dave's problem.

"Phil," she said, "what do you think about Dave and Debbie?"

Phil had turned thirteen only a month before, but he was like Dave, mature in a quiet way. Now he looked very serious. "I knew about it," he said. "I guess I've known forever, or it seems like that. I didn't think he'd ever tell while they were here on the island. I thought he'd wait until they got away where things were easier."

"Maybe he decided things wouldn't really be easier," Ellen said. "Or else, maybe he's stronger now. Do you like her?"

"Oh, sure, I *like* her. But that doesn't change anything."

"What do you mean?"

"She's still an Indian, and things are gonna be rough. Everyone will try to talk them out of it!"

Ellen felt a touch of panic. "Do you think they can—talk them out of it, I mean?"

Phil shrugged again. "How do I know?"

If only everything could be certain and sure and settled, Ellen thought. *Why does life have to be uncertain and unpredictable?*

She carried cookies into the living room, where the conversation was really going very well. Debbie was shy and reserved, of course, but Dave was wonderful. There was pride on his face that no one, Ellen thought, could have resisted. He was proud of this lovely girl he had claimed openly at last, and he was equally proud of his parents for being so kind and courteous and calm.

"Have you thought it all through?" Uncle Archie was saying. "Do you know how tough it's going to be?"

"Yes. But we're willing to face the tough parts. If you two aren't too upset, that'll be the biggest thing," Dave said.

Aunt Betty spoke gently. "It's mostly that we'll hate seeing you get hurt. Because you *will* get hurt, Dave—you, I think, more than Debbie. Every time anyone slights Debbie, you'll feel her pain more than she will. We'll hate it that our children have to suffer. You can see that?"

Debbie nodded. "Grandpa said the same thing. But we—forgive me, Mrs. Ludlow—but we have to live our own lives."

Aunt Betty looked at the girl. "You've had a bad time already," she said. "I feel so terrible that your grandfather's never been found."

Dave and Debbie did not even exchange a look, and Ellen busied herself pouring more pop in one of the glasses.

"It's just as well," Debbie said in her soft voice. "He probably would have wanted it like that. He was old-time in his thinking, and he loved the woods. I think he's all right."

They really weren't going to tell, Ellen realized.

It was going to be a secret known forever to only three people. Well, then, she would lock it in her heart and keep it there.

It was several days before Ellen could bring herself to talk to Aunt Betty about Dave and Debbie. She felt sure that Aunt Betty wasn't really prejudiced but just afraid for Dave, aware that he would meet intolerance all through his life if he married Debbie.

"But could you love her?" Ellen asked. "You and Uncle Archie?"

Aunt Betty nodded slowly. "I don't think it could happen over night, but I think I could learn to love her very much. *You're* responsible for that, Ellen."

"Me?" Ellen looked at her aunt in complete astonishment.

"Yes, you. First, there was your friendship with Rachael. When you kept bringing her here, I got to see more and more that she was just like any kid, sweet and funny and not different. And when you told me about Clarisse, how she'd hurt you, but how you'd both discovered how to be really friends again, I began to think about things I hadn't thought of before. I'm still a long way from being as tolerant as I want to be, but you've taught me a lot."

Ellen sat down suddenly, feeling a little wobbly. It was just simply incredible to her that she could influence anyone, and an adult at that. "Thank you," she said weakly. "I guess that's the nicest thing anyone ever said to me."

"Anyhow," Aunt Betty said, "they're awfully young—in one way, anyhow—and there's a long time to go. But if they continue to feel this way, then Dave doesn't have to worry that we won't accept Debbie. We will. But they'll have a tough row to hoe."

A tough row to hoe. Ellen thought. *Yes, it would be that.* But she had a feeling of certainty in her heart that they would make it—the Indian girl with her grace and beauty and the tall white boy who had developed, it seemed, all the courage he was going to need.

On the day when Miss Numadabi was to announce the people who would be represented in the art exhibit, Ellen went to school with her heart in her mouth, or so she told Mary Ann. Mary Ann who couldn't draw a straight line, found the whole thing a little amusing. But she assured Ellen that she'd get one thing in. Miss Numadabi wouldn't be mean enough to keep her out altogether.

Ellen wasn't so sure. She went to the art room, almost dragging her feet. She had submitted four paintings—two of the view of the lake from her bedroom window, one of the lane rutted with spring mud, and one small watercolor of Washington. The latter was something she had done one night in the winter when she was feeling homesick, and it was not particularly pretty. Oh, the monument was there and the gold dome of the Capitol against a twilight sky, and the spire of the church she belonged to, but there were slums in the foreground, and the whole picture gave out a feeling of loneliness. She was almost sorry she had submitted it. She had another one of the view of the harbor in Little Current that was really better.

Once inside the art room, she began circling the walls, as other kids were doing, looking for something of her own, both envying and admiring the other paintings that had been hung in honored positions. Debbie's painting of the blessing deer was in the most prominent position, as indeed it should be. With the exception of Miss Numadabi, no one else came close to Debbie in artistic talent. Ellen looked closely at it, aware that something in it was different; but for a second, she wasn't sure what. Then she saw it. The boy in the bushes, the boy who had alerted the deer to flight, was no longer dressed in a skin jacket and soft moccasins. He wore jeans and sneakers and a pale tan shirt that blended into the trunks of the trees. His hair was light, and anyone looking at it would know it was Dave.

Ellen realized at once the significance of the change. Not only was Debbie brave enough to admit it was Dave in her picture, but she had repainted him as he really was, willing to accept him as a white boy, not wanting him any different. Ellen felt as though she had been allowed to see a small miracle.

And right next to Debbie's painting was the little watercolor of Washington! Ellen gasped her astonishment and stood staring at the little painting. She looked up and Miss Numadabi was watching her.

"I didn't think you'd want this one," Ellen said feebly.

"It's better than the others," Miss Numadabi said. "Do you know why, Ellen?"

"No. Why?"

"Because you know it with your insides. The paintings of the island are like something on a pretty calendar. You didn't look beneath the surface and see things that aren't beautiful. But the picture of Washington is honest. I can *feel* the city when I look at it."

Ellen stared at her teacher and then back at her little creation.

"The loneliness is there," Miss Numadabi said, "and the ugliness, but the beauty is stronger than anything else. The skyline—the solid curve of the Capitol dome and that fragile church spire, is pure poetry. You must love Washington very much."

Ellen stood in utter stillness while the words exploded in her head. For almost a year she had agonized over what was perfectly obvious to Miss Numadabi. It was true. She did love her home very much. In a way, that was why she hadn't been able to endure the painful and ugly things, because they were like blemishes on something that she wanted to be perfect.

Her mind flew to her criticism of Dave—that he had been content to accept the wrong things on the island and not try to do anything about it. That was what she had done. Dave was right; she had run away.

But now Dave had made a move, he had taken a stand. He had risked everything to try to make one small step toward righting things.

Maybe that's what her friendship with Clarisse was—just one small step toward righting some of the terrible wrongs at home. Maybe her new feeling about the church and her new understanding of what prayer ought to be had been given to her as weapons to use in her small battle against prejudice and hate. It wouldn't be easy but she knew now that she would leave the island when school was over. She was going to go home. Oh, she would come back to the island. As long as she lived, she would come to visit—but only to visit.

She smiled at Miss Numadabi, and she was sure that no one watching her could have guessed that she had just made the biggest decision of her life.

"Yes," Ellen said, "I guess you're right. I love Washington very much. I'm glad you took this one for the exhibit."

That night she walked down to the dock and sat quietly on the edge of it, watching the sunset glow brilliantly across the sky. The calmness that had filled her in the art room when she realized that her heart had already made its decision to go home was starting to shred a little. She was thinking of all the Ludlows and of Mary Ann and Rachael, the kids at school, the teachers, the way the air smelled, and the silence of the stretch of water, and she was beginning to wonder if she could bear to leave it.

But Dave would be going away to school, and Sam and Mary Ann would be getting closer as they got older, shutting out all others. And besides, there was that feeling of obligation about going back. It could be called a need to do what had to be done. In a small way she had done that even here. If she had done nothing more than save Andrew's life, then she had not wasted this year on the island.

And oh, the riches that had been given her—the love of some very special people, a clearer understanding of herself and of what God wanted her to be, a thousand memories of beauty to carry forever in her heart. It had been a good exchange; she had given and received more than she had ever dared hope for. Maybe it would be that way at home, too. After all, there were people there who wanted her, too—daddy and Frances, Clarisse, her other friends—and maybe, just maybe, Stephen Upton.

It was going to be all right.

As clearly as though she held it in her hand, she felt the smooth delicate shape of the little blessing deer. She would put it on her dresser at home to remind her constantly of this year and everything she had learned.

"Thank you, Mr. Wawaskesh," she whispered solemnly across the water. "Thank you for everything."

She looked up to see Dave coming toward her across the lawn. She would tell him first of all, because she knew he would understand completely. It wouldn't matter, really, how many miles stretched between them; they would always share a special love.

"Dave," she called, her voice soft in the spring night. "I've got something to tell you."

He started to run, and for just a second he looked like a young boy running in the blue twilight. It was only when he got closer that she could see that he had become, truly and proudly, a man.